Killing Another

Andrew Leatham

CHAPTER 1

Neither the enveloping warmth of the delivery suite nor the quiet efficiency of the two midwives could do anything to stem the tide of terror that was rising within Kate Lowe. She knew with the instinct that only mothers possess that something was terribly wrong; that her new born baby was fighting to survive. But the two young women — neither of them over 30 — who were desperately struggling to make the baby breathe freely, remained, outwardly at least, reassuringly calm.

One of them even managed a smile as she massaged the tiny body, snugly enveloped in a fluffy white towel, with increasing vigour. After almost a minute, the child showed no signs of losing her intense birth colour in favour of the healthy pink that would indicate her blood was oxygenating properly and a sure sign to the midwives that her survival was not in doubt.

The midwife continued to smile reassuringly but through her smile whispered an instruction to her colleague: 'Better call the paediatric crash team.'

She continued to work on the baby — and maintained her smile — seconds feeling like minutes and minutes like hours as she waited the arrival of the specialist team that right now represented the new-born's best chance of life.

As the infant was carried away, Kate Lowe screamed, 'What's happening? Where are they taking my baby? What's wrong?'

The midwife managed to say, 'There's no need to worry. We're doing everything we can. I'll be back in a minute,' before she too vanished out of the door, leaving Kate and her husband Peter alone, paralysed by ignorance, not knowing what was happening, convinced only that their tiny daughter would not survive.

So they waited in silence, Peter's grip on his wife's hand relentless. A digital clock facing the end of the bed clicked its way through 15 minutes, then 25 minutes and was working its way towards 40 minutes when Peter decided he'd had enough.

'I'm going to find out what's happening,' he said.

But before he could even rise from the bedside chair, the door opened and a tall young man with mousey hair and wearing medical scrubs was standing in front of them.

'Mr and Mrs Lowe,' he began. 'Sorry to have kept you waiting. I'm Doctor Hart. The first thing to tell you is that we've managed to stabilise the baby...'

'Samantha,' Kate burst out. 'She's going to be called Samantha.'

'Yes. Very nice. However, as I was saying, we've managed to stabilise her but she's on a ventilator and we need to keep her there while we do some tests.'

'What kind of tests? What's wrong with her?' insisted Peter.

Dr Hart ruffled his hair with his right hand, as if searching through his brain for an answer, but the action was actually nothing more than a nervous gesture.

'That's what we're hoping to find out,' he replied. 'We think she may have some kind of heart defect which is causing her breathing difficulties.

'We'll know more when the tests are complete but I'll be honest with you — your daughter is a very poorly little girl and until we know exactly what's causing her problems I can't be sure of the outcome.'

'She's going to die. She's going to die isn't she?' The question rose in an anguished cry from Kate's throat. 'Tell me. I want to know the truth.'

'Mrs Lowe I can't tell you any more than I already have because right now I don't know any more. We need the test results before we can be sure of anything but I can tell you that Samantha is not in any immediate danger. The ventilator is breathing for her so I suggest you concentrate on getting a good night's sleep. We may know more tomorrow.'

'We want to be with her,' said Peter. 'We want to see her. Can we see her now?'

'Not at the moment. Maybe tomorrow. In the meantime, I'll get some accommodation sorted out for you both.'

The door closed quietly behind him.

Breakfast in the hospital canteen was not something either of them was looking forward to. St Mary's Hospital for Women and Children in Manchester may have world-class expertise and excellent facilities for its patients but it was still part of the National Health Service and that meant budgets, especially when it came to food. It was only a few minutes after 8.00am but already the constituents of the 'Full English' — bacon, sausages, fried egg, mushrooms and grilled tomato — were showing signs of age on-set. Peter and Kate settled for a bran cereal, plain yoghurt and fruit. Their window seat overlooked a main road, which allowed them to bridge the silence between them by taking an apparent interest in the mundaneness of the outside world — students making their way on foot to the nearby Manchester University; people queuing for buses and commuters in cars searching in vain for shortcuts to avoid the congealing traffic.

An hour passed before a nurse appeared and without introducing herself said simply: 'Mr and Mrs Lowe? Would you come with me please? Dr Hart wants to see you.'

'How's Samantha? Is she any better?' asked Kate, gathering her belongings and shuffling to her feet.

'Dr Hart will tell you everything he can,' the nurse replied primly. 'This way.'

They took a lift to the fifth floor then turned left along a corridor painted pastel pink and passed several doors until they came to one affixed to which was a small brass plaque that read: 'Dr Alan Hart. Neonatologist.' The nurse tapped once, opened the door and said: 'Mr and Mrs Lowe,' before stepping aside.

Alan Hart sat behind a desk with an unprepossessing view of other hospital buildings to his left. Still wearing the same scrubs from the night before, unshaven, black bags weighing down his eyes, he had the unmistakable look of a man who hadn't slept.

'Mr and Mrs Lowe. Good morning. I hope your accommodation was OK,' he said, rising and extending his hand to them both. 'The good news is that Samantha remains stable, although she's still on the ventilator. However, I have to tell you that we've got the preliminary test results back and I'm afraid it's not encouraging.'

'Oh my God. I knew it. She's going to die isn't she?' cried Kate, her eyes glazing with tears.

'Not if I can help it Mrs Lowe. However, as I told you last night, she is a very poorly girl. We need to carry out a couple more tests to confirm our suspicions but if we're right, she's going to need surgery. But there's no need to worry, we have some of the best paediatric surgeons in the world in this hospital and they will do an excellent job. Samantha really couldn't be in better hands.'

Blank expressions stared back at him, as if neither of them had understood a word he had said. He was on the verge of repeating himself when Peter, his face unchanged, spoke.

'So what's wrong with her? You haven't told us what's wrong with her.'

'Well, as I said, the preliminary test results show…'

'Just tell us what's wrong with her. We want to know,' his voice rising as his hands began to tremble.

'We're pretty certain she has a rare heart condition known as Ebstein's Anomaly. In layman's terms it means one of the chambers of her heart is enlarged, bringing about a corresponding reduction in another chamber and muscle loss. The net result is that not enough blood — and therefore not enough oxygen — is reaching the baby's lungs.

'It can be repaired but the surgery is very complex. It involves reconstructing the valve between the two damaged chambers which, as I'm sure you can appreciate, is something akin to a work of art on a child so small.'

Neither of the Lowes looked at each other and for a few seconds neither spoke as they struggled to absorb the implications of the doctor's words.

'Will…will it…Will this operation save her life?' asked Peter, emotion straining every nerve in his face.

'If it is successful, I think she can look forward to leading a pretty normal life, yes.'

'What do you mean, if it's successful?' asked Kate.

'Mrs Lowe you have to understand that all surgery carries some degree of risk. We try our utmost to reduce that risk but in cases such as this we cannot eliminate it completely. You have to be aware of that before we proceed.'

'And what happens if you don't operate?

'Then I'm afraid Samantha's life will be short and painful.'

'When would you want to do the operation?'

'Well Mrs Lowe, in anticipation of you agreeing, I've already spoken to our head of paediatric surgery and she's willing to do the operation tomorrow morning.'

'Tomorrow? But she'll only be... She's too small... Surely. She's too small.'

Peter simply put his arm around his wife's shoulders and pulled her close.

'Samantha's in our new-born intensive care unit,' said Dr Hart. 'You can look at her through the window but I can't let you go in to her because of the risk of infection. I'll get the nurse to take you along. It's only at the end of this corridor. And let me know whether you want to stay here again tonight or whether you want to go home. Samantha's on the list for 10 o'clock tomorrow morning so I should be able to tell you more by, say, 2 o'clock.'

Later, neither Peter nor Kate would be able to recall exactly what they did in the following 25 hours but by 10.00am the next day, they sat arm-in-arm in a corridor outside the operating theatre suite while the life of their new-born — and only — child hung finely balanced in the hands of strangers.

A few minutes after 2pm Alan Hart emerged from the operating suite with a woman in her mid-30s, still wearing a surgical cap and gown, with the mask casually pulled down over her throat.

'Mr and Mrs Lowe, this is Keely Jeffris, our head of paediatric surgery. She's just finished operating on Samantha.'

'Hello, pleased to meet you,' she said, the Australian accent strong. 'And I'm delighted to be able to tell you the operation has been a success.'

Kate did not hear whatever came next as she collapsed in a flood of tears on Peter's chest.

'Does that mean she's going to be OK?' he asked.

The surgeon threw an anxious glance at Hart. 'Come to my office and we'll explain things in private.'

Once his secretary had served coffee, Hart rocked back in his chair, his fingertips together.

'Mr and Mrs Lowe. The operation carried out by Keely and her team has been a success. However, that isn't the end of the matter. You see, Ebstein's Anomaly — which is what Samantha had — is also associated with a condition called Wolff-Parkinson-White Syndrome which, in a nutshell, causes the heart to beat irregularly and very, very quickly and that has its own problems.

'At the moment we don't know whether Samantha has got WPW Syndrome but it's a fairly safe bet to say she probably has. Now, we can treat this complaint with drugs. The downside to that is that she will have to take lots of drugs regularly for the rest of her life.

'And there is always the possibility that her WPW becomes so bad that drugs can no longer actively control it. If that happens there is only one course of action. A heart transplant.'

Before Hart's words had sunk in and certainly before either of the Lowes had the chance to react, Keely Jeffris spoke.

'Bearing in mind the current state of Samantha's heart and the scarcity of paediatric organs for transplant, I suggest we put Samantha's name on the waiting list immediately.'

CHAPTER 2

Seven Years Later

The first fearful wail came a few seconds before eight minutes after midnight. Kate Lowe could be so precise because her eyes opened to the glow of a digital clock exactly as Samantha started to cry; a cry that gave vent to all the horrors of a child's nightmare; a cry that every parent has heard and is powerless to prevent. After seven years of watching her every move, listening to her every breath, Kate was finely in tune to every nuance of her daughter's behaviour.

And this was a first.

Almost before the dreadful ululation had subsided, Kate was at Samantha's bedside, holding her close, cradling the sobbing child in her arms.

'It's alright darling. It's just a bad dream. Mummy's here. Sshh.'

But the soothing words failed to stop Samantha's trembles and tears, brought on by the terrors of her dreams.

'I'm scared Mummy. What was it? I didn't like it.'

'I told you,' said Kate in her best, quietest, most calming voice. 'It was only a bad dream. Nothing to worry about. Everybody gets them, even me and Daddy. I know they're scary but you're perfectly safe.

'Now, close your eyes and go back to sleep. I'll stay here with you. Everything's alright.'

Gradually, the sobbing and the shaking subsided and Samantha drifted off to sleep once more. Kate, wearing only the towelling robe she had grabbed as her left her own room, snuggled in close, partly to reassure her daughter and partly in a bid to keep warm.

After 20 minutes or so, she had managed to squirm her way under the duvet where she too fell fast asleep.

Then it happened again.

It had been two weeks since Samantha had come home from hospital and eight weeks since she had received the heart transplant that saved her young life. Her parents dreamed the operation would mend all her ills and that the family would be able to lead a normal life, or at least, a life more normal than they had been leading.

They dreamt of no more daily cocktails of drugs. They dreamt of no more weekly visits to the hospital so that the doctors could monitor their daughter's condition. They dreamt of family holidays; of rough-and-tumble games; of swimming and running together. They dreamt of just being ordinary.

At first, the drugs had been pretty successful at controlling her abnormally fast heartbeat, dizzy spells, palpitations and breathlessness. Samantha was frail and unable to do many of the things other kids did but she accepted her lot with graciousness. She never complained and spoke constantly of a time 'When I'm better.'

But one day, out of the blue, things got worse.

Peter Lowe had been at work when he took a call on his mobile to say that Samantha had collapsed at school and had been rushed to hospital.

He didn't stop to tell his boss. He simply fled from the office and leapt into his car, ringing his wife from his mobile phone as he steered one-handed along the busy dual carriageway towards the hospital.

The panic-stricken pair arrived at Manchester Royal Infirmary virtually together, dumped their cars without paying the parking fee and fled into the Accident and Emergency Department.

They found Samantha in a cubicle, sitting up in bed looking drained but smiling and hooked up to a heart monitor.

'Oh darling. Are you OK?' Kate gathered her daughter in her arms. 'What happened?'

'We were outside the in the playground. It was playtime. I was playing hide and seek. Then everything just went black.'

'Have you hurt yourself? How do you feel now?' asked Peter anxiously.

Before the child could answer a young doctor stepped into the cubicle. 'Ah, you must be Samantha's parents. I'm Dr Rashid,' he said. 'I pleased to tell you that she's OK.

'We think she just fainted and luckily she didn't hurt herself when she fell. But I also have to tell you that I've had a look at her medical records and I'm concerned that her Wolff-Parkinson-White syndrome is no longer being adequately controlled by the drugs.

'For that reason, I want to admit her to the Children's Hospital for observation and some tests.'

'What are you saying? What's wrong with her?' the panic rising in Kate's voice.

'I'm sure the doctors who have been looking after Samantha have explained everything to you Mrs Lowe but, put simply, I think we've reached the stage where drugs alone are not enough to keep the WPW in check.'

'And that means what, exactly?' Peter asked.

'Well, I'm not a paediatrician Mr Lowe, nor am I a heart specialist but I think we may have to consider the possibility of a heart transplant.'

Kate dropped onto the bedside chair as if someone had cut off her legs at the knees. Peter stood open-mouthed, the colour draining from his face.

'She...she's...she's. She's been on the waiting list since she was a few days old,' he finally managed to mumble. 'How urgent is it?'

'I'm not qualified to answer that Mr Lowe. The priority will be determined by the paediatric cardiologist.'

The call, when it came, was free of drama, urgency or panic. Free, in fact, of all the anxieties that Peter and Kate Lowe had imagined.

The first contact was a text message one Saturday morning to Peter's mobile, asking him to ring the Royal Manchester Children's Hospital urgently.

The person who answered his call told him calmly that a suitable heart had become available and that Samantha was to be taken as quickly as possible to Wythenshawe Hospital, on the outskirts of Manchester, the heart transplant centre for the North West of England.

In readiness for just such a call, the Lowes had packed two overnight bags, one for Samantha and one for themselves and it was with a feeling approaching anti-climax that Kate now loaded them into the boot of the family car while Peter made sure their daughter was securely strapped into the back seat.

They were at the hospital 40 minutes later and less than an hour after that, Samantha was being prepared for surgery.

Waiting around in the corridor close to the operating theatre only served as a reminder of how many hours they had spent in similar situations over the past seven years. This time it seemed that they waited an eternity but, in reality, it was something just over five hours before a man in an expensive looking dark suit emerged from within the theatre complex.

'Mr and Mrs Lowe?' he asked. 'I'm Marcus Thomson and I'm the consultant paediatric cardiac surgeon here at Wythenshawe. My team and I have just completed the transplant operation on your daughter and I'm delighted to tell you we have every reason to believe it will be a complete success. I expect Samantha to make a full recovery.'

Kate's reaction was to sob deeply and uncontrollably, a mixture of relief and happiness, while Peter just wanted to grab hold of Marcus Thomson and kiss him.

'Thank you doctor, thank you, thank you,' he bumbled. 'I can't tell you how grateful we are. Thank you, thank you.'

'My pleasure,' replied Thomson. 'And I'm a Mr not a doctor. I'm a consultant.'

'Sorry, yes, thank you doctor, thank you,' Peter went on, the correction not even registering.

'Now, is there anything you want to ask me before I go back to my little patient?'

Through her tears Kate asked the question every recipient's family wants answering: 'Whose was it? Whose heart has Samantha got?'

'I'm afraid we never reveal donor's names Mrs Lowe,' said Thomson. 'It's not medically ethical and I believe it could be psychologically damaging to both families. We will tell the donor's family that their daughter's heart has been used to save the life of another little girl, but that's all.'

'So another little girl has died to give our Samantha life?' asked Kate.

'No Mrs Lowe. You daughter has been given the heart of another little girl who sadly passed away and her family thoughtfully donated her organs to save others. She did not die specifically so that your daughter could live.'

Peter just managed to stop himself giving voice to the thought that rushed through his mind. In a milli-second he decided it wouldn't achieve anything and could permanently damage their relationship with the hospital. His thought was: 'Patronising bastard.'

Samantha's second scream shocked her mother awake, her arms already entwined around the child's shaking body.

'Hush, hush, hush. It's okay. It's just another bad dream.'

'Make it stop Mummy. I don't like it. It frightens me.'

'I know sugar but everything will be alright, I promise,' said Kate. 'You just go back to sleep. There's nothing to be afraid of. Everything will be better in the morning.'

But the next night it happened again. And on the night following.

On the fourth night, Kate lifted Samantha from the bath and was towelling her dry, trying at the same time not to weep at the sight of the vivid red scar that ran vertically down her daughter's chest and would remain visible for the rest of her life.

'Will the lights come again tonight Mummy?' a bewildered little voice asked. 'I don't want them to. They're not nice.'

'Try not to think about them darling. I'll make you a nice warm cocoa with milk. That'll help you sleep.'

'Make them go away Mummy. I'm frightened.'

'Everything will be alright darling. Daddy and I won't let anything hurt you. You're safe and sound.'

But the lights did come. Three times that night.

They continued to visit their horrors upon the child for another three nights before Kate decided enough was enough and took Samantha, unannounced, to the local GP's surgery.

The receptionist had been polite but firm. No appointment, no doctor.

Kate had been equally polite but forceful.

'You can tell your doctors that I'm here and I'm staying here until one of them has a look at my daughter. She needs help and I'm not leaving 'till she gets it.'

Almost an hour passed before a man approached her. He was tall — well over six feet — greying at the temples and dressed in a weary-looking tweed sports jacket with leather trims around the cuffs and a line of pens in the breast pocket. He was also wearing what appeared to be moleskin trousers. On his feet were a pair of brown brogues, so highly polished they could have been used for mirrors. A pair of large, round, horn-rimmed glasses reduced his eyes to the size of peas, giving him the appearance of a praying mantis.

'Mrs Lowe? I'm Dr Hillman. Sorry you've had to wait so long. We don't normally see people without an appointment but I understand you were very insistent. Do come through.'

Taking Samantha by the hand, Kate followed the doctor along a short corridor, past several rooms until they came to one with his name on it.

'Do take a seat,' said Dr Hillman, indicating a chair at the side of his large oak desk and pulling up another for Samantha.

'Now, what appears to be the problem?'

The first thing that struck Kate was that Dr Hillman was probably not as old as his dress and demeanour indicated, as if he were somehow cultivating an image of age and experience.

Although the computer screen on his desk displayed Samantha's entire medical records, the doctor listened patiently as Kate told him of her daughter's need for a heart transplant; where and when it was done; when Samantha had been allowed home and when the nightmares had begun.

She told him how they recurred and how much the child was frightened by them. Now she was beginning to be frightened by them too.

'I see,' was all he said.

Turning to the child, he went on: 'Samantha, I bet you're fed up with doctors but I just need to ask you a few questions so I can work out what to do to help you with these bad dreams. Is that all right?'

Samantha bit her bottom lip and nodded.

'Tell me about these dreams. Is it the same dream every time?'

'Yes.'

'And what happens? What do you see?'

'Lights.'

'Lights? What kind of lights?'

'Ones that move. Very bright ones.'

'And what colour are they?'

'All sorts. Red, white, orange. And sometimes green and blue.'

Hillman's brow creased in a puzzled frown before he went on: 'Do you only see lights or is there something else too?'

'Music. And singing.'

'What kind of music?'

'Just music. Like Daddy plays in the car.'

'Is it nice music?'

'I don't know. I can't hear it properly because of the other noise.'

'And what does that noise sound like?'

'I don't know. It's just a noise. Very loud. All the time.'

'Okay Samantha. You're doing very well. Just another thing. Why does this dream frighten you?'

'Because I can't move.'

'Why can't you move?

'I don't know. I just can't. I can't move my arms or my legs.'

'Do you know where you are when you're in this dream?'

'No. I always try to shout for my Mummy but I can't do that either.'

'Do you know why you can't?'

'No. I try to shout but nothing comes out.'

'Thank you Samantha. You've been very brave. Now, I'm just going to have a little chat to your Mummy. Is that Okay?'

'Yes.'

Hillman, who on close inspection Kate had decided was probably not much more than late 30s, spoke softly as if he did not want Samantha to hear what he was saying.

'Mrs Lowe, I don't think there's too much to worry about. Samantha's had a very traumatic time these last two or three months and it's bound to have some effect on her little mind.

'I'm going to give you a mild sedative to help her sleep and see how she goes. If she continues to have these dreams bring her back and I'll see what else we can do. We might have to enlist some specialist help.'

As he was speaking he was inputting something on his computer keyboard. He hit another button and a printer next to his left hand spewed out a prescription which he folded and handed to Kate.

She stood to leave, stumbling out a 'Thank you' as she did so.

'My pleasure Mrs Lowe, but just one thing. If you do have to come back and see me, please call and make an appointment. It's much easier for everyone.'

'Yes doctor. Thank you.'

After her bath, Peter read Samantha a bedtime story while Kate made her a cup of cocoa and prepared the sedative, following the instructions to the letter. Half an hour later, Samantha was asleep.

The minutes after midnight, the time when Samantha's nightmare usually returned, came and went and the Lowes settled down for their first undisturbed night's sleep for a week.

It was four o'clock in the morning when the lights came back. Bigger, brighter and more terrifying than ever.

CHAPTER 3

Dr Hillman was sympathetic but not particularly helpful. In fact, Peter Lowe described their second visit to his surgery as a 'bloody waste of time.' He had listened attentively while Kate had described how at first they thought the sedative had worked but how it had actually only delayed the nightmare. She told him how it had been worse than previously; how Samantha had been absolutely terrified; how she refused to go back to sleep.

When she'd finished, the doctor inputted something into his computer and hit the print button.

'Mr and Mrs Lowe, I can understand how distressing this must be for you, for all of you. But my inclination is still that these nightmares are nothing more than an after-effect — a hangover, if you will — of what Samantha's been through recently.

'I'm sure they'll stop eventually. She just needs time, you'll see. But in the meantime, this' — he handed Kate a prescription from his printer — 'is a stronger sedative to help her sleep. There's enough there for 14 nights. It should do the trick.'

'Do either of you two want something to help you sleep?'

'No thanks doctor,' said Peter. 'If Samantha's sleeping, then so are we.'

That night, for the first time in almost two weeks, the Lowe household slept undisturbed. But it wasn't to last.

The lights came back to Samantha the following night and the night after that and the night after that and continued to visit her until her screaming and crying almost became the norm for her parents. For Peter, at least, it became just one more painful thing in his daughter's young life; just one more thing she had to live with; just one more thing he had to live with.

And then there was the night the lights changed.

They came earlier than usual, before the clock ticked past midnight into the following day. They came with their brilliantly flashing colours; with their muffled music; with the underlying, unidentified sound. They came with all the terrors that they had previously visited upon the petrified child. But this time they came with more.

This time, they came with faces.

By the time Dr Hillman's surgery opened at 8.30am, Peter, Kate and Samantha Lowe were waiting on the doorstep. This time, there was no hanging around. Hillman swept them straight into his consulting room and told the receptionist to reschedule his appointments because he was going to be at least half an hour late.

Samantha sat on her father's knee as she told the doctor about her scary new nightmare. How this time she had seen faces mixed in with all the lights and the sounds. Her mother supplied the additional, probably unnecessary, information that Samantha had been so scared she'd wet the bed.

'Okay Samantha. Is it alright if I ask you some questions like last time?' asked Hillman. 'There's nothing to be worried about. Your Mummy and Daddy are both with you, so nothing's going to happen to you. But I need you to tell me what you saw so I can help you.'

'Okay.' Her voice barely audible.

'Now. Did you recognise these faces? Did you know any of them?'

'No.'

'Were they boys or girls? Or were they grown-ups?'

'I don't know. They weren't proper faces.'

'How do you mean, they weren't proper faces?'

'They didn't have noses or eyes or anything.'

'So how do you know they were faces?'

'I just do. One of them was saying something.'

Hillman's expression gave nothing away but his brain registered the fact that here was a small child who probably needed psychiatric help.

'And can you tell me what the face said?' he asked gently.

'Not really. But I think she was saying "Don't".'

'You said "She." So you know it was a she.'

'I think it was. It sounded like a girl's voice.'

'Did the face say anything else?'

'No.'

'How many faces did you see? One, two or more?'

'I don't know. They just kept coming and going and I was frightened. I tried to shout for Mummy but nothing came out.'

'I remember you telling me that the first time. You also said you couldn't move. Could you move this time?

'No.'

'Thank you Samantha. I don't think I need to ask you anything else. You've been very brave.'

He turned to Peter and Kate. 'You probably won't like what I'm about to suggest but believe me, I wouldn't suggest it unless I thought it was absolutely the right thing to do.

'I want Samantha to see a child psychiatrist.'

Peter exploded.

'A psychiatrist?' he yelled. 'You saying my daughter's nuts? There's nothing wrong with her. She's as bright as the next kid. I'll have you struck off, you bastard. You know nothing.'

Hillman remained unruffled by Peter's outburst. 'Mr Lowe, please calm down. I'm not saying for an instant that there's anything mentally wrong with Samantha but there is obviously something buried deep in her subconscious that's troubling her greatly and I'm afraid I'm not qualified to find out what it is.

'That's where the child psychiatrist comes in. They work with teams of other experts in child health and between them they have a much better chance of helping Samantha than I do.

'They'll work with her to identify the problem and devise a plan to rectify it. It's not a quick-fix solution and I'm afraid the nightmares will probably continue for some time yet. But I do believe it's in Samantha's best interests. Will you at least give it a try?'

Before Peter could answer, Kate spoke for him. 'Yes, of course, doctor. We'll do anything we can to help her, won't we Peter? What do we need to do?'

Hillman replied: 'Thank you Mrs Lowe. Actually, I know a chap called Stephen Parke who is the consultant child psychiatrist at the Children's Hospital. I'll give him a call and see if we can get you an appointment as quickly as possible. I can see this situation is distressing for all of you and I want to do everything I can to resolve it.'

Conditioned by television and films to believe that psychiatrists' offices were dark, sombre places, full of ancient wood and creaking leather furniture with dusty floor-to-ceiling bookcases, Peter Lowe was pleasantly surprised at Stephen Parke's surroundings.

The sober suit with matching tie that he was programmed to expect was also missing. Parke, casually but expensively dressed, looked like a man on holiday.

Although he had been carefully and completely briefed by Hillman and had conscientiously read all of Samantha's medical notes, he listened earnestly as Peter and Kate recounted every step of their daughter's life, from the moment of her birth up to last night's nightmare.

As they spoke, he made comprehensive notes that, as well as snippets of information about what they were telling him, included comments on their body language, their apparent attitude towards their daughter and towards what was troubling her.

At the end of it, he asked to spend some time alone with Samantha. He settled her comfortably in a huge, green, beanbag and sat beside her on a low, blue upholstered stool.

He spent 15 minutes asking her exactly the questions that Martin Hillman had asked and made careful notes of her answers. A later comparison would show the answers were identical.

After the session was over and the Lowes had made an appointment to return at the same time the following week, Stephen Parke began the task of compiling his case notes. These included all the information that Martin Hillman had provided, plus his own observations, which concluded that Samantha's nightmares appeared to be the result of a trauma, as yet unidentified; that she was deeply loved by both her parents, who were anxious to discover the cause of their daughter's problems. And that it was highly unlikely she was being abused within the home.

For the next session, Parke asked to be alone with Samantha again and once more settled her into the big green beanbag.

He spent a long time talking to the child about her school, her friends, what she enjoyed doing, her favourite pop star, the kind of music she liked, what she did at home, where she went with Mummy and Daddy.

When he thought he had established a trust, he broached the subject of her nightmares and, yes, she was still having them. Every night.

'Tell me Samantha, do you still see the same things or have they changed?' he asked.

'A little bit.'

'How? What's changed?'

'I can see the little girl now.'

'Is this the same little girl you told me about last week? The one you said you thought was saying "Don't"?'

'Yes.'

'And when you say you can see her, tell me what you mean.'

'I can see her face and stuff.'

'That's really interesting. Tell me what you can see.'

'She's a bit older than me and she's got red hair. Mine's blonde.'

'What does she look like, can you tell me?'

'She just looks normal, you know.'

'Yes. You're doing really, really well Samantha. Is there anything else you can tell me about her?'

'No. She comes and goes and comes back again. Sometimes she comes right up to me, very close. I don't like her. She frightens me.'

'Why do you think that is,' asked Parke. 'You said she was normal. What is there to be frightened about?'

'She's crying and she wants something. But I don't know what it is. I can't tell what she's saying. But it must be important because she's very upset.'

'Samantha, do you think that the little girl could be you?'

'No it's not me. I told you. She's got red hair and mine's blonde. And besides, she's older than me.'

'Okay. That's really good,' Parke told her. 'I think we'll leave it there. Just one more thing. When you first spoke to Dr Hillman you told him that when you had these bad dreams you felt like you couldn't move. Can you move in the dreams you're having now?'

'No.'

'Why do you think that is?'

'Because I'm tied up.'

At the third session, Parke introduced Peter, Kate and Samantha to Richard Fairfax who, he said, was going to help him try to unravel Samantha's nightmare, to see what sense could be made of it, to see if its origins could be identified.

Fairfax and the child were left alone.

The child psychoanalyst began in exactly the same way as Parke, talking calmly and quietly to Samantha, gently probing into her life yet at the same time establishing a trust.

Eventually he produced a set of crayons and a thick wad of drawing paper and asked her to draw for him. First of all, she drew Mummy and Daddy. Then she drew the house they lived in, a smart post-war semi-detached, just over the city boundary in Cheshire. She drew her school, her school friends and her teacher before Fairfax asked her to draw what she saw in her nightmare.

She drew a box with two smaller boxes inside it, one on each side. Then she scribbled all over it with vivid slashes of orange, to which she added jagged flashes of white, green, red and blue. When she'd finished, she pushed it across the table towards Fairfax.

He studied it intently for a moment before asking: 'Samantha, where are you in this picture?'

A small finger pointed to the middle of the box.

'You're in there?'

'Yes.'

'Do you know what it is?'

'No.'

'When you spoke to Dr Parke last week, you told him you thought you were tied up. Are you tied up in the box?'

'Yes.'

'Thank you Samantha. You've been a very good girl. I'm very happy to have met you and I'm looking forward to meeting you again. I love your pictures. You can take them home if you want, but can I please keep this one?'

She did not understand the significance of what she'd drawn and readily agreed.

As the Lowes made their way back to the hospital car park, Richard Fairfax and Stephen Parke sat down together to discuss Samantha and what was troubling her.

They agreed that the boxes made no immediate sense as a descriptor of what Samantha was seeing every night. Maybe the significance of the boxes was masked by their childish simplicity. They also agreed that the vivid splashes of colour could indicate anger. Anger at being unable to move; anger at being unable to make herself heard? Neither man wanted to speculate at this early stage. Both agreed that they needed to spend more time with the tormented youngster to coax more information from her.

It was weekend and Fairfax was relaxing at home, thumbing through the pages of the Daily Telegraph, bringing himself up to date with events nationally and internationally when his eyes let upon a headline on a single column story.

It read: 'Child Murder Police Hunt Van' and went on to detail how West Yorkshire detectives, investigating the murder of 12 year-old Kylie Morris, were appealing for anyone who may have seen a red Ford Transit Connect van, which they believed may have been used to abduct the girl from a street near her home in Bradford.

She had been found raped, bludgeoned and left for dead in a field near Otley, more than 10 miles away, three weeks earlier.

He finished reading the paper, glanced at his watch, and decided it was time to walk his dog the four miles over the moor to the neighbouring village and a liquid lunch in the Ancient Shepherd.

His route took him along a well-marked path, over a stile in a dry stone wall and across the top of a small, long-abandoned quarry to a point where he had to negotiate another stile and cross a moorland road. For reasons he never understood, his dog hated this stile, steadfastly refusing to climb over it, leaving Fairfax with no option but to lift her over.

The spaniel tumbled from his arms and was brought up short by her lead as Fairfax climbed over the stile to join her. As he did so, he heard the sound of an approaching vehicle and turned round to see a medium-sized van which, as it passed, he noticed was branded Ford Transit Connect. The name failed to register.

The Ancient Shepherd was, as usual for Saturday lunchtime, full; the clientele its usual eclectic self. Plumbers rubbed shoulders with lawyers. Farmers and accountants traded stories and insults. All of them harangued the landlord. The Ancient Shepherd was the great leveller. No one cared who you were, what you did or how much you earned. Just being there was all.

Fairfax had forgotten the Daily Telegraph story and could not have recalled the name Kylie Morris if his life depended on it. Samantha Lowe was not on the radar.

It was mid-way through his third pint when an image of the van he had seen on the moorland road flashed inexplicably through his mind. He was struck by its compactness. By its shape. By its boxiness.

He wondered, briefly, whether it was as boxy looking inside. And he felt the colour drain from his face.

'You all right Richard? You look like you've seen a ghost,' asked one his companions.

'What? Yeah, yeah. I'm fine. I just need some air, that's all.'

Outside, the cool September air concentrated his mind. He thought again about Samantha Lowe and the picture she produced when he asked her to draw what she saw in her nightmare.

A box with two smaller boxes inside it.

Now he understood.

The inside of a van with two front seats.

He thought about the other marks she'd made on the drawing — and everything fell into place.

The vivid slashes of orange were street lights; the other colours headlights, traffic lights, neon signs.

The unidentified noises were the engine note and the hum of tyres on tarmac.

The music came from the radio.

In her nightmare, Samantha Lowe was tied up in the back of a van speeding into the darkness.

He reached into his inside pocket for his mobile 'phone to call Stephen Parke.

CHAPTER 4

'It's an interesting theory Richard.' Stephen Parke was trying his best to manage his colleague's sudden enthusiasm. 'But do you honestly think it has any firm basis in reality. Couldn't it just be coincidence? Don't forget, it was only yesterday that we agreed this case needed more input from others.'

'I know that,' replied Fairfax. 'And I know that what I've just told you is nothing more than my interpretation. The important thing is that Samantha's nightmares are capable of that interpretation. And right now that's the best solution we've got. I think it's something that bears further investigation.'

'If that's how you want to proceed...What are you proposing? I think we have to be very, very careful. We're dealing with a seven year old child don't forget.'

'I'm aware of the risks Stephen but I want to help this child. Why don't I spend the rest of the weekend pondering the best course of action, then you and I get together on Monday?'

'Okay. My office about 11 o'clock?'

'Fine. See you then.'

Back at the bar, the Ancient Shepherd had suddenly lost its attraction. Fairfax could not get Samantha Lowe and her nightmares out of his mind. He drained his pint and instead of ringing his wife to collect him, set off on the four mile walk home.

By the time he arrived, the skeleton of a plan was swimming around in his head. It stayed there throughout the following day, fluctuating, shifting and transforming so that by the time Monday came around, it had metamorphosed into being, to his mind, the only way forward.

That night, just like every other night in the past weeks, Kate and Peter Lowe spent around an hour persuading Samantha to go to bed; persuading her that she was safe; persuading her that nothing could harm her. That night, just like every other night in the past weeks, the terrified child would only agree to go to bed if Kate went with her and slept with her in the same bed. And that night, just like every other night in the past weeks, Kate was awakened not long after midnight by her daughter's screams; a penetrating, painful cry followed a few seconds later by the warm, spreading dampness as Samantha wet herself.

Samantha had tossed and turned, resisting sleep at all costs until, eventually, exhaustion closed the mantle of slumber around her. But in her fitful sleep, the nightmares returned once more to haunt her. In the half-light radiating from the novelty night light — a giant red and white toadstool — plugged into a wall socket, Kate was aware that tonight Samantha was sitting bolt upright, shouting at something she perceived to be at the end of her bed.

Some of the child's words were mumbled, indistinct, indecipherable to a brain shocked into consciousness. But others were plain and unmistakable. The ones Kate would vividly remember were 'No,' 'Please,' 'Don't hurt me' and 'I won't tell anybody.'

The words, interspersed with sobs and whimpers, signalled to Kate that something had changed; the nightmare was not the same; it had somehow got much worse. She tried to exclude her immediate thought but couldn't. No matter how hard she tried, the thought kept repeating itself.

It was as if her daughter was pleading for her life.

Downstairs, swaddled in a warm, dry duvet and embraced in her mother's arms Samantha became calmer and finally stopped crying. Neither of her parents pressed her to reveal the vision that had caused her so much fear. The experience of the past months had shown them that left alone, she would eventually volunteer the information.

And so it proved to be that night.

'Mummy, there was a man,' she began.

'Where darling? In your bad dream?'

A tremulous, hesitant voice continued: 'Yes. It was horrible. I didn't see the little girl. I just saw this man. He had something in his hand. I don't know what it was but I know it was bad.'

'How do you mean bad, sweetheart. How was it bad?'

'He was going to hit me with it. I was screaming at him not to do it but I knew that he would.'

As usual, Stephen Parke's secretary offered Richard Fairfax tea and the choice: 'Earl Grey or builders.' And, as usual, he chose builders, disliking the perfumed after-taste that the aromatic concoction left in his mouth. Parke chose Earl Grey and both men subconsciously decided not to get down to business until the tea arrived, choosing instead to make small talk.

Conversation ranged over the Ancient Shepherd, the football results and the prospects for the week's weather until the phone on Parke's desk interrupted; a single elongated tone, indicating it was an internal call.

Parke listened. 'In that case you'd better put her on,' was all Fairfax heard his colleague say.

'Mrs Lowe, good morning,' said Parke.

For the next few minutes, Fairfax was party only to one side of a conversation in which Parke tried to be reassuring and calming. Eventually he said: 'Actually Mrs Lowe, Richard Fairfax is with me right now. Is there any chance you could bring Samantha in to see us right away?'

An unheard response.

'Excellent. Just come straight up. I'll tell my secretary to alert reception that you're expected.'

All three of the Lowes had the black-eyed, baggy skinned, sallow complexions of people who hadn't slept for a very long time. Samantha also had the red-rimmed eyes of someone who had shed a lot of tears. Sympathy flowed freely from the medical men until they suggested that perhaps Peter and Kate would like to go for coffee while they spoke to Samantha alone.

Over the next hour, the pair of them gently probed here, prodded there while, through a mixture of words and drawings, Samantha Lowe laid bare her latest night-time terror. By the time they had finished, Samantha was mentally and physically exhausted —'She looked like a wet rag,' her mother would recall — but Parke and Fairfax both believed they now had a greater understanding of the little girl's problem.

And, unspoken, each of them had reached the same horrifying conclusion.

As the Lowes waited hand-in-hand for the lift that would return them to the outside world, the two men sat on opposite sides of Parke's glass and chrome desk scanning the copious notes they had made during the interview.

Parke spoke first. 'Well. What do you think?'

Fairfax weighed his answer carefully. 'It's a difficult one. Your original report on Samantha said her problems were caused by a trauma which, at that time, was unknown but I think this morning we've come pretty close to identifying what it could be. I think she's being attacked.'

The china cup rattled in its saucer as Parke put it down. 'I was thinking the same thing, except I don't think it's Samantha that's being attacked. It's someone else. The girl she saw in her earlier nightmares probably. That girl is somehow manifesting herself in Samantha's subconscious.'

'That would explain the inconsistencies in her story,' replied Fairfax. 'The way she said the girl she saw wasn't her and then went on to say it was her tied up inside the box she drew; the box that could now be a van.

'If we're right, it begs the question, who is the little girl in Samantha's nightmare and what happened to her?'

'Well, right now we don't have a clue do we?' replied Parke. There was a pause as he considered very carefully what he was about to say. It was as if the words didn't want to come out his mouth; that by venting themselves they would make something unthinkably terrible come true.

Finally, he said quietly: 'I really, really don't want this to be true, but I think that what Samantha is seeing, experiencing almost, is much more serious than an attack. I think she is experiencing the murder of another child.'

There. He'd said it. It was probably enough to earn him the ridicule of his fellow professionals and downright derision from the man on the opposite side of his desk but it was what he now believed. He waited for the howls of scorn.

Fairfax looked at him with an expression that could have been relief, or gratitude, or a mixture of both.

'I'm glad you said that first,' was Fairfax's response. 'I was trying not to say it, but I'd reached pretty much the same conclusion. I agree with you. Who she is and why it's happening I have no idea, but in her nightmare, Samantha is being killed.'

CHAPTER 5

The reception had been in full swing for more than an hour when Richard Fairfax arrived. It was the kind of event he hated but it was also the kind of event at which attendance was more or less compulsory — it involved the hospital being given money. This one was the launch of a partnership with the University of Manchester and Manchester City Council in which the city council would fund a programme of research into the effects of poverty on child development.

The only saving grace to the proceedings was that it was being held amid the architectural splendour of Manchester's Victorian Gothic town hall in an area known to all town hall workers as 'The Bees.' This was the large open space just outside the main entrance to the Grand Hall, where the two sweeps of the magnificent main staircase met. It was tiled in hand-thrown white tiles some of which were decorated with golden bees, the symbol from Manchester's heraldic coat of arms that signified its place in the vanguard of industrial development.

As he reached the top of the wide stone staircase, a waitress stepped forward proffering a tray of champagne. He took a glass and looked around for a friendly face, his ears battered by the cacophony of conversation from the assembled mix of academics, medics and local politicians.

He had exchanged pleasantries with a couple of people he didn't know, had a brief conversation with a professor from the university he had met a couple of times before and was seriously trying to devise an escape route from the whole event when a voice to his left said: 'As I live and breathe, Richard Fairfax. And I do believe it's your round.'

He knew instantly who it was.

'Hello Charlie,' he said turning to meet the owner of the voice. 'Who let you in? They told me this was an up-market do.'

Charlie Boone was *The Times* staff reporter in Manchester and a walking caricature. Or at least, that's how he was popularly described, although a caricature of exactly what had never been properly identified.

A little under six feet tall, Boone had the kind of frame on which clothes merely hung. Even the best tailor in the world would struggle to make him look smart. 'His clothes fit where they touch,' a friend had once said, not unkindly. He did not appear to possess a shirt without a frayed collar or a tie that was unstained. An unruly mop of black hair, shot through with patches of grey, topped off this unkempt appearance, giving him the air of a neglected Old English sheepdog.

'I think I'm on pretty safe ground if you got through the door. How you doing you old rogue?'

Richard could never remember the exact circumstances under which he met Charlie Boone, although they had been acquaintances — rather than close friends — for a number of years. He had occasionally given the journalist a hand with a story, sometimes being quoted by name and at other times merely as 'a source.' And three or four times a year they would meet for lunch and a forgotten afternoon in one of the city's many good old fashioned pubs that have survived the onslaught of expensive chrome and glass establishments that prefer to describe themselves as 'bar' or, pretentiously, 'lounge.'

The journalist and the medic made easy conversation while they both drank another glass of champagne.

'Do you know what Richard?' asked Boone eventually. 'These kinds of events bore the arse off me. Fancy a pint? We could nip down to the Brits.'

No more persuasion was necessary and five minutes later the pair of them walked into The Briton's Protection, having passed under the ever-watchful gaze of Oliver Cromwell, whose portrait adorned the pub sign swinging over the front door.

The narrow bar and the two comfortable 'snugs' were packed with concert-goers enjoying a drink before heading off across the street to the Bridgewater Hall, the city's premiere concert venue and home to the world-famous Hallé Orchestra. But by the time Boone had squeezed his way to the bar and ordered two pints of Robinson's best bitter, the place was virtually deserted with only a dozen or so drinkers still remaining. It was as if the rest of the crowd had been swept away whereas, in reality, the concert was about to begin and they had simply rushed off to take their seats. Many of them, Fairfax knew from experience, would be back at the interval.

Fairfax always enjoyed his occasional drinking sessions with Boone. The journalist was good company, a born raconteur, who kept Fairfax and anyone else within ear shot, entertained with tales of the human foibles, follies, misdemeanours and transgressions that were his stock in trade.

Tonight was no exception. For close on half an hour Fairfax did nothing but grin, chuckle, laugh out loud and order more beer. Boone was in good form.

And then came a story that deeply affected Richard Fairfax, child psychoanalyst.

Boone took a long draught of his Robinson's: 'I did a tale last week about a bloke in Wrexham who reckoned he'd turned into a violinist after he'd had a liver transplant. Seriously. He honestly believed his new liver had given him the ability to play. Reckoned he was tone deaf before the op but after it, he's a regular bloody Mantovani. Mad as a March hare undoubtedly but he genuinely believed it. He was trying to find out whose liver he'd got because he's convinced the donor was a musician.

'It didn't make the paper because the news desk said it was too *Daily Mail*, whatever that might mean. But it turns out the old fiddler might have been on to something. I had a look on the old worldwide interweb thingy and there's dozens of stories like my man in Wrexham and more than one medico — American, of course — who supports this theory called cellular memory.

'The theory is that memory isn't just in the mind; it exists in all organs of the body and can be transferred along with whatever lump of your insides is being transplanted. Depending on whose liver, kidney, heart or whatever it is you're getting, you could possibly inherit some of the donor's talents as well.

'So there you go Richard. All you need is one of my kidneys and you too could be witty, charming, scruffy and an Olympic standard piss-artist. Not that one of my kidneys would be much use to man or beast mind you. Same again?'

Fairfax spent a restless night, his brain unable to let go of Charlie Boone's words: 'Memory isn't just in the mind; it exists in all organs of the body.' It was a truly fantastic theory. How could a function of the brain reside in a kidney or any other major organ? But it did offer a possible clue to the ordeals that Samantha Lowe was suffering. Or did it? Wasn't he just falling for a crackpot theory merely because it offered him a glimmer of hope? Samantha had undergone a heart transplant though. And she had suffered a significant behaviour change as a result.

Just after 5am, with further sleep impossible, he pulled on his bathrobe, padded through to his study and when his laptop had booted up, keyed the words 'Cellular Memory' into his search engine. In less than one fifth of a second, the computer returned more than 18 million results.

Fairfax went downstairs to the kitchen, made himself a large, strong coffee and settled down to read.

Two hours and two more coffees later, at about the time he would normally be rising to face the day, Richard Fairfax had read enough to be able to put his argument to his colleague Stephen Parke. He switched off the laptop, went next door to the bathroom and stepped into the shower.

As the cascade of hot water pounded his body he ran over what he had learned. Boone had been right about the theory of cellular memory. The notion was that every cell in the human body had its own chemical 'mind' so if these cells were transferred — for example in an organ transplant — the 'mind' would also be transferred to the new host.

Although medical science had still to accept the theory, there was a stack of anecdotal evidence, particularly about people who had undergone heart transplants, and plenty of researchers busily trying to prove that cellular memory really did exist. Two of them, scientists Gary Schwartz and Linda Russek of the University of Arizona, had already written a book in which they proposed: 'all systems store energy dynamically . . . and this information continues as a living, evolving system after the physical structure has been deconstructed.'

Schwartz and Russek had teamed up with Paul Pearsall, a psychoneuro-immunologist — which Fairfax interpreted as a psychologist who studies the relationship between the brain and the immune system — to carry out a study of 10 cases in which a heart or heart-lung transplant had been carried out. The study consisted of in-depth interviews with the recipient, their families and friends and also the donors' families and friends.

All of them gave compelling evidence to support the theory of cellular memory but the most forceful of all, thought Fairfax as he towelled himself dry, was that of an 18-year-old boy who wrote poetry, played music and composed songs, and was killed in a road accident. A year after he died his parents came across an audiotape of a song he had written and called 'Danny, My Heart is Yours,' which told how he 'felt he was destined to die and give his heart to someone.'

The 'Danny' who received his heart turned out to be an 18-year-old girl, named Danielle. When she met the donor's parents, they her played some of his music, including 'Danny My Heart is Yours.' Despite never having heard the song, she knew the words.

In another case, a seven-month old boy had been given the heart of a 16 month-old who had drowned. The donor suffered from a mild form of cerebral palsy which affected mostly the left side of his body. The recipient, who had not displayed any symptoms of cerebral palsy before the transplant, developed the same stiffness and shaking on his left side.

Fairfax knew that Parke would be sceptical but he was determined to argue his case. And to reinforce it, he would use a quotation he had come across during his brief research. It came from the 19th century American psychiatrist and philosopher William James and it said: 'To disprove the law that all crows are black, it is enough to prove one single crow to be white.'

Samantha Lowe would be his white crow.

Sceptical didn't quite cover Stephen Parke's reaction when Fairfax explained the theory of cellular memory, the anecdotal evidence to support it and how he believed it fitted with the experiences of Samantha Lowe. Flabbergasted; dumbfounded; astounded; speechless — all were more accurate descriptions of how he received the information. He listened in complete silence, a look that was a mixture of puzzlement and incredulity spreading slowly across his face as Fairfax continued to spout.

When he'd finished, Parke stared at him blankly, slowly turning a cheap plastic ball-pen through his fingers, struggling to find an adequate response. Eventually he settled for: 'Richard, tell me you're not being serious. This is a joke isn't it?'

Fairfax looked like a small boy who'd just had his favourite toy confiscated.

'No it's not,' he said, barely disguising the hurt in his voice. 'I'm very serious. Yes, it's an unproven theory. Yes, it's off the wall. And yes, it might sound like a completely crackpot notion. But it fits.'

'Think about it Stephen. Samantha Lowe spent the first seven years of her life leading a relatively normal existence, untroubled by nightmares until she underwent a heart transplant. It was only after the transplant that her problems began, which would indicate to me that there's a link between the two.

'And let's face it, we have no idea whose heart Samantha was given. Just suppose the donor died a violent death...

Parke butted it. 'I think that's stretching things a little Richard...'

'But suppose it's true. Suppose Samantha's heart came from a victim of...'

'You're just inventing circumstances to fit your theory.'

'No I'm not. And you have to admit that it is a possibility. You can't dismiss it out of hand. You can't prove where her heart came from any more than I can. Can you? All I'm saying is that we have a theory — and I'm putting it no higher than that, a theory — which could explain what's happening to a terrified young girl and I think it's worthy of further investigation.'

'Alright. If I was to support you — which I must qualify as not being the same as agreeing with you — how do you see things progressing?'

Fairfax visibly eased in his chair, his shoulders noticeably relaxing. When he spoke, his voice was at a lower pitch.

'Well, we need to establish exactly how the donor of the heart came by his or her death. But I think the first priority is to talk to Mr and Mrs Lowe.'

CHAPTER 6

Locals liked to describe their swimming baths as 'Victorian,' despite the fact that it featured none of the architectural elegance, elaborate decorations or stained glass which characterise public pools of the period. In fact, the pool, in a suburb of Bradford, once capital of Yorkshire's woollen industry, had been built by a local mill owner in the early years of the 20th century in an apparent act of philanthropy towards his workforce. But Jabez William Fryer had another motive in paying for the pool, solidly built in stone, with a green and white tiled interior and 30 individual changing cubicles around three sides of its 25 yard long pool, carefully marked into four lanes by lines of black tiles.

Jabez was well aware of the respiratory diseases that plagued wool mill workers. He had seen men and women die in agony, literally gasping for their last breath. And he had concluded that the healthier he could keep his workers, the more productive they would be and the more money he could make. Forking out a few thousand pounds on a swimming pool therefore struck him as an eminently sensible investment.

His workers, who comprised 95 per cent of what was then a village, were entitled to one free swimming session a week. After that, they paid a penny, just like the handful of swimmers who were not in the employ of Jabez William Fryer.

Today, more than 100 years after it first opened, the pool was as popular as ever, although admission was now the equivalent of more than a week's wages working in Jabez's mill. There were public swimming sessions early every morning, at lunchtime and again in the early evening. School groups used the pool; the local swimming club held training sessions there two nights a week; a sub-aqua club used it for introductory dives once a month and every afternoon, when school was over, the pool ran swimming lessons for youngsters of all ages and all abilities.

Kylie Morris had been a regular at these lessons since she was seven years old. Five years on she was an accomplished swimmer but still enjoyed her twice weekly lessons, during the course of which she had mastered all the principle strokes — front crawl, back crawl and breaststroke — and could even do a passable length of butterfly. She had been taught racing dives and tumble turns. The water held no fear for her.

And now the new instructor had taken a special interest in her. He encouraged her to push herself; to strive for more power; to go faster. He had even mentioned that with the right training she could be good enough to one day swim for her country. In fact, Robert Craymer was so keen to help the little girl to succeed, he had offered to give her free coaching for an hour every Saturday morning. All she had to do, he told her, was to persuade her Mum to bring her to the pool. At the age of 12 Kylie was too young to understand the true nature of his apparent beneficence. And her mother was too overwhelmed by pride to see it.

So every Saturday for the last two months Kylie had ploughed up and down the pool doing endless lengths while Craymer —'Call me Bob' — lavished attention upon her mother, occasionally yelling encouragement to his young protégé.

Closer to 40 than she was to 30, Tracey Morris had taken care of herself. Despite having three children, of whom Kylie was the eldest, assiduous work in the gym had helped keep her trim and toned. Her naturally black hair, cut in a simple shoulder-length style, shone with the lustre of wet coal. She shunned the fashions of her age group, preferring instead to opt for younger styles, a choice which had earned her the insult 'Mutton dressed as lamb' from more than one of her contemporaries. But the overall result was that Tracey Morris could still turn heads; could still attract admiring glances. Many of which had come, unseen by her, from Robert Craymer.

The affair had started simply enough. It began with Craymer inviting Kylie and her mum for a coffee in a local cafe after Saturday training so they could discuss Kylie's progress 'in comfort.' From the cafe it was but a short step to the pub, at first in the early evening, so that Craymer could discuss with Tracey elements of Kylie's coaching over a quick drink. Early evenings developed into later ones and more drinks.

It wasn't long before Tracey realised she was becoming more and more attracted to this athletically built, charismatic man who seemingly wanted nothing more than to nurture her daughter's talents in the pool. She told him of her hopes and desires for her daughter; how she hoped that sport would be a passport to better things, just as it had for so many. She told him of marriage at the age of 21 to a young soldier who was invalided out of the army after being wounded by a sniper's bullet in Belfast. She told him how her husband had adapted to life in Civvie Street and become a lorry driver and how he did regular runs to the Continent, a job which meant he was away from home more often than he was at it. She told him how that had meant she had brought up the three kids virtually single handed.

It was only later, when people started asking questions, that she realised that conversation with him had been a one-way street. She knew almost nothing about Bob Craymer. He was undoubtedly a Yorkshireman, she could tell that from his accent. He told her he was 42 and that he lived 'out Heaton way' on the other side of the city. But apart from that she knew nothing. He had never spoken of his family. He had never spoken of his past. He had never spoken of where he came from or what he had done with his life. And she had never asked.

In the gossip pages of the tabloids and in the few trashy paperbacks Tracey had found time to read; married women who embarked on affairs were put on pedestals; worshipped; lavished with gifts; whisked away for secret trysts in luxurious hotels.

Tracey's affair was different.

It seemed to consist entirely of a few drinks in a pub well away from where she lived, followed by unprotected sex in the back of Craymer's old car, parked up in lonely, unseen places. There was no pedestal; no gifts; no luxurious hotels and the closest she ever came to being worshipped was a once-whispered: 'Has anybody ever told you you're a bloody good shag?'

With the benefit of hindsight, she should have realised from their very first liaison that this was an affair that was never going to take flight. As usual, her husband was somewhere on the Continent so she told Kylie she was going to play bingo with a friend, made her promise to lock the door and not go out, then hopped on a bus into the town centre.

At Craymer's suggestion, they arranged to meet outside a multi-storey car park but by the time she had walked there from where the bus had deposited her, she was five minutes late. And there was no sign of Craymer. With no means of contacting him — he claimed he didn't own a mobile — the only choices she had were to wait or leave. Waiting won although the longer she stayed, the less it seemed like the best idea. With each minute that passed she felt more and more like a hooker touting for business and had just decided to head back to the bus station when an old car, streaked with grime and blotched with rust, pulled up. Craymer was behind the wheel and motioned for her to get in.

As she did so, he leaned across to kiss her, slipping his hand inside her coat to feel her breast as he did so. She moved backwards to avoid his lips, pushed his hand away and snapped: 'Don't.'

The rest of the journey was spent in near silence as he drove to a pub out of town. Not out-of-town as in driving to one of the dozens of pretty pubs in the countryside that surrounded the conurbation, but as in out-of-Bradford. When the car stopped, Tracey recognised she was in the outskirts of Bingley outside an undistinguished local pub, where they spent the next two hours drinking and talking about nothing consequential. At one point, she did think to ask him whether he was alright to drive after so much beer but let the moment pass.

Leaving the pub, they went to a fish and chip shop, eating their food in the car out of polystyrene boxes with little plastic forks, not quite the romantic dinner-aux-deux she had dreamed of, a feeling of a disappointment only reinforced when Craymer threw the empty wrappings on to the back seat.

Driving back towards Bradford, he made a diversion into an unlit industrial estate, where he found a secluded spot and switched off the engine. He launched himself over the gear lever and handbrake and she felt herself pinned into her seat by his weight. She responded to his kisses and for the first time that night was beginning to feel excited, like being a teenager on her first date all over again. This time she didn't complain when he slipped his hand inside her coat, unbuttoned her blouse and fondled her breast. But when he tried to slide his hand up her skirt she heard herself crying: 'Don't.'

'No Bob. Don't,' she protested. 'Not yet. It's too early.'

'Whaddya mean it's too early?' he grunted.

'It just is,' Tracey replied. 'I mean...I will...Just not now. Not here.'

Craymer muttered something inaudible under his breath, fastened his seat belt and started the engine. 'Right then. Best be off,' he said.

Twenty minutes later, he dropped her outside a taxi office about three miles from her home and said: 'I'll see you at the pool.'

He didn't even offer her the £5 cab fare.

The affair was brief. Less than three months after it began, Tracey suddenly woke up to the fact that she had put everything she ever held dear — her children, her husband, her home — on the line for a few stolen hours of illicit sex.

The next time she met Robert Craymer she told him it was over. Not knowing how he would react, but guessing it could be explosively, she chose to tell him in the pub in the hope that the proximity of others would dampen his fury. In the event, Craymer took the news calmly, almost as if he was expecting it. He told her he understood when she said she had been foolish; that she had been flattered by his attentions but that he would never mean as much to her as her family. He told her he respected her decision and that loving someone sometimes meant knowing when to let go.

They finished their drinks and parted. Tracey's last words to him were: 'Bob, I hope we can still be friends and I still want you to coach Kylie...'

Craymer drove away from the pub, his anger rising within him. How dare that bitch treat him like that? No woman ever turned her back on Bob Craymer. He used them and he disposed of them and he went on to the next one. That's how it worked. They didn't dump him. He'd show the bitch.

By the time he reached the shabby terraced house where he lived alone, the need for revenge bubbled from every pore of his body.

And he knew just how to take it.

CHAPTER 7

It was a group of mountain-bikers who found Kylie Morris, naked, her hands bound behind her by two strong plastic cable ties, with a length of grey duct tape forming a crude gag. She had seemingly been thrown over a dry-stone wall, dumped like a sack of garbage, by the side of a lonely road on The Chevin, the heavily wooded escarpment that overlooks the pleasant little town of Otley.

She had been beaten so badly around her head and face that she would be barely recognisable even to those who loved her most. But she was alive. Hyperthermic and clinging to life by the slenderest of threads but alive all the same.

Within half an hour doctors in St James's Infirmary, Leeds, were battling to save Kylie's life, thanks to the Yorkshire Air Ambulance service, one of whose MD-902 helicopters was based at Leeds-Bradford Airport, less than two miles from where the mountain-bikers had found her. The fact that the medics could not immediately put a name to the battered, broken child was the least of their worries.

Kylie's hysterical mother had reported her missing 36 hours earlier when she had failed to turn up for her regular evening swimming lesson. The first call had come from Bob Craymer who had asked simply whether Kylie was unwell. Tracey Morris felt her heart stop. For her, every mother's worst nightmare loomed large.

In desperation she called all of Kylie's friends that she knew, but none had seen her since she left school heading for the swimming pool.

Police made an immediate appeal for anyone who may have seen the little girl to come forward and issued a photograph of her; a typical school portrait, smiling, hair neatly brushed, face scrubbed until it shone.

But not a single soul came forward.

The appeal was repeated at a Press conference the following day, which resulted in a crop of time wasters and cranks calling in. But of Kylie there was still no news.

The young policewoman appointed as Family Liaison Office tried her best to keep Tracey calm and up to date with what was going on but there was precious little to report.

Police forces across Europe had been alerted to watch out for Kylie's Dad who was driving a truck full of car parts back from Italy. Kent Police had been asked to pick him up at Dover ferry port and rush him home under blue lights. There was nothing positive.

Then came the 'phone call.

Tracey was only aware of the policewoman saying: 'Yes, yes,' 'Of course,' 'I understand' and finally 'Yes. Straight away.'

Putting the 'phone back in her pocket she said calmly: 'Mrs Morris, I need you to come with me to the hospital. A badly injured little girl has been admitted...'

Before she got any further Tracey was verging on the hysterical once more. 'Is it Kylie? Is it her? How bad is she? I need to be with her.'

'Mrs Morris, please try to stay calm,' said the police officer. 'You must remember that there's a chance it's not Kylie. We need you to tell us. We need to go to the hospital now.'

By the time the pair reached A&E, Tracey could barely stand. Her body sagged under the burden she was carrying, so the policewoman — a slightly built blonde who said her name was Rosie — sat Tracey down and went to the reception desk.

A few moments later a man in dark blue medical scrubs appeared and introduced himself to Rosie as the A&E consultant Dr Michael Hallworth.

'Look, I'm afraid this is going to be very difficult,' he said. 'We've got Kylie on a life support machine but the fact is, her brain stem is dead. There's nothing more we can do for her.'

Rosie tried to keep a professional detachment. 'I see...'

'Well, actually, we need to establish whether this little girl is Kylie Morris as quickly as possible. Because if it is, she's on the NHS Organ Donor Register.'

'Oh! Christ doctor. I can't broach that with her. Not in the state she's in.'

'Don't worry about that,' said Hallworth. 'If it is Kylie, a team of specialists will take over. But we'll wait until the father gets here before we take it any further. For now, I just plan to tell her Mum that she's in a coma and that we're doing all we can for her.'

At the sight of her precious daughter linked to the life support machine, lights blinking, electronic traces rising and falling and a faint but clearly audible 'bleep,' Tracey Morris sank into an ocean of tears. She grasped her little girl's hand and sat there sobbing, saying nothing, the devastated, distraught, uncomprehending expression on her face conveying her grief more eloquently than a million words.

And there she stayed, unmoving and unmovable.

Frank Morris's heart sank when a Customs officer waved him over as he drove his 40-tonne articulated truck off the ferry at Dover. And it sank even further when he saw two policemen approaching. A feeling of guilt gripped him, not that he had done anything wrong. His load was perfectly legal, his paperwork in order and — as far as he knew — there were no illegal immigrants hiding in the back. Nevertheless, he felt his heart rate rising as one of the policemen opened the driver's door.

'What's the problem officer?' asked Frank.

Neither man offered an answer; instead they concentrated on establishing his identity from his driving licence and passport.

'What's going on? I need to know,' demanded Frank.

The taller of the two calmly replied: 'I'm afraid your daughter Kylie has had an accident of some kind. We've been sent to take you to her.'

'Christ. What happened? Where is she? Please...' Frank was beginning to crumble in his ignorance.

'We don't know the details of exactly what happened,' said the policeman. 'All I can tell you is that she's in intensive care at St James's Infirmary in Leeds and that's where we're taking you now.'

'But what about my truck? It's got a valuable load.'

'Don't worry about that Mr Morris. Your employer is sending another driver to collect it,' the policeman said. 'Now, if you'll come with us please...'

As soon as Frank had fastened his seatbelt in the back seat, the patrol car started to move and the car's observer switched on the blue flashing light array on the roof. It stayed on until the car stopped outside the hospital four hours later.

Tracey was still clutching Kylie's hand, silently praying for a miracle when the doors to the Intensive Care Unit opened and she heard a familiar voice: 'Oh, Tracey. What's happened? How is she?'

She rose, still sobbing and threw herself into the arms of her husband. 'She's in a coma, Frank. She's in a coma.'

'But how? Why? The police wouldn't tell me anything. They just said she was badly injured.'

'Because some bastard did it to her Frank,' she replied. 'She's been beaten senseless. Look at her. Just look at what they've done to my baby. I should've been there. I should've have met her at school. She'd have been alright then.'

'Tracey you can't say that. You can't blame yourself. And anyway, Kylie's the most important thing right now. What have the doctors said?'

'Just that they're doing all they can. But look at her Frank. She's just lying there. Why don't they do something?'

'Mr and Mrs Morris, I realise this is extremely distressing for you...' Neither of them had heard the ward door open. Nor had they heard Dr Hallworth enter. But there he was and he was accompanied by two other men, both of whom wore the same dark blue scrubs. 'But we have to do some tests. So if you don't mind, I need you to just leave for a few minutes. It won't take long.'

'Tests? What for? She's in a coma.' Frank Morris was trying to keep himself under control.

'It's just routine. To help us establish a prognosis. I'll come and talk to you when we're done. Why don't you wait in the canteen?'

The next hour was lost to them as they sat in the garishly lit canteen, each with a cup of tea untouched and growing cold, desperately trying to make small talk, anything to take their minds of what was happening to them. A slightly embarrassed Rosie, the Family Liaison Officer, simply sat and listened while two floors up Dr Hallworth watched as two of his senior colleagues carried out the tests laid down in the guidelines used by every NHS hospital, on every potential organ donor, to establish that death had occurred.

They began by shining a torch into both of Kylie's unseeing eyes to see whether the light triggered any kind of reaction. Then they used a piece of cotton wool to stroke the cornea — the transparent outer layer of the eye which in life is extremely sensitive — to see if the eye reacted in any way. Next, they applied pressure to the little girl's forehead and pinched her nose, looking for the slightest hint of a movement in response. Ice-cold water was then injected into each ear, an action which would cause eye movement in a living person, and then gently inserted a thin plastic tube into her windpipe to see if that provoked coughing or a gagging response. Finally, they switched off the ventilator for a few minutes to see whether Kylie made any attempt at breathing on her own.

When none of these actions prompted even the slightest response, they carried them out a second time to completely satisfy themselves that the battered, broken body before them had suffered — as the guidelines stated — 'irreversible loss of the capacity for consciousness and the irreversible loss of the capacity to breathe' and that this state was not due to drugs or hyperthermia.

At that point Dr Hallworth sent a nurse to collect Kylie's parents. She took them to the brightly decorated but subtly lit Relatives' Room where they found Dr Hallworth waiting with a smartly dressed, middle-aged woman, her auburn hair done up in a complicated looking French plait. The medic made no attempt at introductions.

He began: 'Mr and Mrs Morris, I'm very sorry but there's no easy way to tell you this. We've done some tests on Kylie and I'm sorry to have to tell you that her brain stem function has ceased.' He paused and a keen observer would have noticed him quickly bite his bottom lip, but in the tension of the intensive care room it went unseen.

'I'm afraid she's dead.'

For a few seconds a silence fell on the room as the couple's brains struggled to absorb the news they had just been given. Then Tracey let out a primeval wail that was neither scream nor cry, but a long-buried primitive sound of mourning.

'No. She can't be. She was breathing,' exclaimed Frank. 'We saw her. You saw her. Her chest was going up and down and everything.'

Hallworth had been here before. 'Mr Morris, I can appreciate what you say but the simple fact is that your daughter's breathing is being done by machine. What you saw is the machine breathing for her. She cannot do it for herself. Kylie has suffered irreversible brain stem death and there is absolutely no prospect for recovery.'

'I don't believe you. I want another opinion.'

'Mr Morris, you can have as many opinions as you want but they will all say the same thing. Sadly, Kylie is dead. All you can do now is authorise me to switch off the life support.'

'And what if we don't?'

'Her heart will stop beating in a few days, despite the fact the machine is still breathing for her. It's an inevitable consequence of brain stem death.'

'So there really is nothing we can do?' Frank was clutching at straws, hoping beyond hope that if he questioned the doctor's judgement long enough, maybe his daughter could be miraculously saved.

'No, I'm afraid there's nothing more you can do for Kylie,' replied Hallworth. 'But there is something you can do for somebody else.'

'What? What're you talking about?'

Half turning to the woman on his left, Hallworth went on: 'This is Mrs Pendleton. She's the hospital's transplant co-ordinator.'

'Transplant?'

But before Frank could get out another word Vicky Pendleton took over.

'Mr and Mrs Morris, I know how difficult this is for you. You've just been told your beautiful daughter is dead and now you think I'm going to start pestering you. Well I'm not. But were either of you aware that Kylie had registered herself with the NHS Organ Donor Register?'

Frank and Tracey stared blankly at each other and Tracey's face dissolved once more into a mask of tears.

'No. No we weren't. But she was only a kid,' said Frank.

'It's not unusual for children to join the register Mr Morris,' said Mrs Pendleton. 'In adults, registering your name is taken as consent for organs to be used for transplantation. But in children the law requires us to obtain the consent of the parent or guardian. So I need to ask you whether we can have your consent.'

Suddenly Tracey stopped sobbing, lifted her head and sat bolt upright, a look akin to resignation on her face.

'She's a thoughtful girl my Kylie,' she whimpered. 'If she joined the register she must have done it because she wanted to. She would've thought about it and decided. And if that's what she wanted, the very least we can do for her now is to grant her wish.'

Vicky Pendleton rapidly looked from one parent to the other, trying to judge the reaction to Tracey's statement. Unable to discern one, she asked: 'Is that both of you giving consent?' Frank, shocked at his wife's sudden assertiveness, stunned by his daughter's desire to be a donor, simply nodded his head. 'Yes. Yes it is.'

'Thank you both so very much. I know it's never an easy decision but you have no idea how much it will mean to so many people.'

And with that, Vicky Pendleton rushed from the room.

Half an hour later and 40 miles away in Manchester, Peter Lowe received a text message asking him to ring the Royal Manchester Children's Hospital urgently.

CHAPTER 8

'Whatever did we do before sat-nav?' mused Ray Wilson. 'It's not that long ago that we'd never have found this place in a month of Sundays.'

'Yeah we would. We'd have stopped and asked somebody. Y'know, a bit of interaction with the public?' Jan Holroyd had a reputation for speaking her mind and not always appropriately.

But Detective Chief Inspector Ray Wilson was growing in his regard for his detective sergeant. She was his kind of copper. Forthright, outspoken, with no time for the politics of the job, she just wanted to get on with it, free from what she saw as interference from those at the top who demanded that things were done this way or that way; that targets were met.

Having spent all his life — and a large part of his career — in the flat, featureless, East Anglian Fens, Wilson was just getting used to the sweeping, dramatic landscape of West Yorkshire; the multi-cultural vibrancy of its towns and cities; the blunt openness of its people; his new force and his new rank.

That's how he came to be getting out of his car on this particular Saturday evening at The Chevin, a wooded beauty spot above Otley, charged with investigating the murder of Kylie Morris, aged 12.

A police car was parked at an angle blocking the narrow lane, and beyond it black and yellow tape demarked an area inside which a team of people in all-enveloping white plastic suits were busily examining every square inch in microscopic detail.

As Wilson and Holroyd ducked under the tape and its 'Do Not Cross' warning, one of the plastic suits broke off from his work and walked towards them. As they met, the suit gave a cursory, 'Hi Jan,' to DS Holroyd and extended his hand towards Wilson. 'You must be DCI Wilson. I'm Martin Garvey, in charge of this rabble of crime scene investigators.'

Wilson brushed aside any attempt at small talk. 'Good to meet you. Call me Ray. What've you got?'

'Not much I'm afraid. There were six guys in the party that found her at around eight this morning. They were out mountain biking apparently. One of them jumped over the wall to take a leak and almost landed on her. Then the air ambulance paramedics were on scene. Virtually nothing's been preserved.'

'Bloody typical,' said Wilson.

'In fairness,' replied Garvey. 'She was still alive when they found her. Their priority was getting her to hospital. Preserving a crime scene probably didn't even enter their heads. That said the paramedics did have the presence of mind to bag up the cable ties and the duct tape that she was tied up with.'

'At least it's something to start on,' put in Jan Holroyd.

'And we've got a tyre track,' added Garvey. 'It's in the grass verge a few metres from where the body was found. We've taken a cast and we'll do some comparisons when we get back to the lab.

'Apart from that, it's what you'd expect. A few blood stains on the grass and some spots of blood on the wall, but that could have happened when she was dumped over it. There's no sign of her clothes or any kind of weapon.'

'Which would indicate she was beaten elsewhere and dumped here,' said Wilson.

Garvey replied: 'Not necessarily. It could be that she was battered here and the attacker took the weapon and her clothes with him.'

'Surely there'd be blood spatter if he'd done that wouldn't there?' asked Jan, trawling up her limited knowledge of forensic investigation.

'Depends what he killed her with and how badly she'd been beaten before she got here,' said Garvey. 'There's not much more I can tell you right now.'

'OK,' said Wilson. 'I think we've seen enough here. Who's doing the post mortem?'

'John Skuse. Good bloke. First class pathologist. You should find him at St James's.'

By the time the detectives arrived at St James's Hospital in the middle of Leeds, Dr John Skuse had completed his examination of the remains of Kylie Morris but was still in the mortuary. He took them back into the examination room where the body was lying on a stainless steel table that, with its channels and drain holes, closely resembled a giant kitchen draining board. Death had drained the lividity out of the mass of bruises and cuts that marked Kylie's face but it remained obvious that she had been subjected to a horrific beating.

'As you can see, she was given a severe and, I would say, prolonged beating, probably on more than one occasion in the hours before her death,' said Dr Skuse. 'There are other bruises on her chest, abdomen and back that are consistent with her being hit repeatedly, probably with a fist. Like a punch bag.

'No doubt about what caused her death though. Blunt force trauma to the back of the head. Probably with a piece of unplanned wood about 75 millimetres square.'

Wilson and Holroyd both gave him a quizzical look.

'I found some splinters in her hair and scalp and there's bruising at the base of the skull that indicates the size of the timber,' he responded, the question unasked.

'The muscles of the shoulders and upper arms are torn, indicating that the weight of her body had been taken upon them for a considerable period. I would say this child had been hanging by her arms.

'And she'd been raped. There are bruises to the inner thigh and some vaginal tearing but there were no semen deposits so I'm assuming that whoever did this wore a condom. Quite an odd thing to do.'

Holroyd gave voice to her thoughts: 'Unless he knew enough not to leave any traces.'

Wilson was struggling to maintain professional detachment, a desire for retribution rising within him.

'Dr Skuse, is it possible to give us some idea of how much time elapsed between the fatal blow being struck and her being certified dead?' he asked.

Skuse pondered for a few seconds. 'Not with any degree of accuracy. Her life was certainly prolonged by the actions of the air ambulance paramedics. But within these walls I would say that the blow was probably struck immediately prior to her being dumped. And the extent of her injuries is such that I doubt she could have survived for much more than an hour without the medical attention she received.'

The implications of his statement were not lost on the detectives.

Kylie had been battered around the head and dumped, naked, in broad daylight. The risk of being seen was extremely high, even though it had been relatively early. The killer either had to be completely crazy, or utterly cool. Or just simply careless.

'Anything else we need to know doctor?' asked Wilson.

'Just one thing. It's not really relevant to the cause of death. But the body had had its major internal organs removed when I received it.'

Internal organs removed. The phrase triggered a flashback in Wilson's memory. A particularly disturbing and upsetting memory that he still struggled to suppress. Internal organs removed.

'Are you OK Mr Wilson?' The voice of Dr Skuse was hollow in his ears, floating in as if from far away. 'You've gone very pale. Do you want some fresh air?'

'No. No thanks doc. I'll be fine. Don't know what happened there,' said Wilson, trying to forget once more. 'Sorry, you were saying there were no internal organs...'

'Yes. It seems that Kylie had put her name on the NHS Organ Donor Register and her parents agreed to organ donation. I understand her heart went over the Pennines to Manchester, her liver to Kent, her kidneys to Cornwall and Edinburgh and her lungs to Belfast.

'As I said, luckily their removal had no impact on the autopsy or my findings.'

All the way back to his car the phrase 'Internal organs removed' looped through Detective Chief Inspector Ray Wilson's brain. He didn't say a word to Jan Holroyd until the pair of them had fastened their seat belts.

'I don't know about you,' he said, staring straight ahead. 'But I could do with a drink.'

As the clock ticked inevitably towards midnight, Ray Wilson was still trying to hypnotise himself with a bottle of single malt and rubbish television. But Dr Skuse's seemingly harmless phrase — 'The body had had its major organs removed' — wouldn't go away. The more he tried not to think about, the faster it repeated in his head.

His move to West Yorkshire had not simply been an opportunity to move up a rank and join a bigger force. It was also an escape. An escape that he knew he would never fully achieve. The cottage he had bought in one of the myriad of moorland villages to the west of the Leeds-Bradford conurbation was slightly larger than the one he had sold in Cambridgeshire. It stood alone at the edge of the village, solidly built in local stone with a roof of Yorkshire flags and a long, gently sloping back garden that gave uninterrupted views of the surrounding Pennines. It spoke silently of shelter, of refuge, of defence against the worst the world could throw its way. But it could offer none of those things against what was going on in Ray's mind.

'The body had had its internal organs removed.' The phrase had instantly conjured up a picture in his head; a picture of a young, intelligent, articulate woman who he had asked for help and with whom he had fallen deeply and irretrievably in love. A woman whose brutal, violent death he saw as his fault. She had been the Curator of Egyptology at the Fitzwilliam Museum in Cambridge when, as a DI on the Cambridgeshire Police Arts and Antiques Unit, he'd asked for help in unravelling the mystery of what appeared to be an ancient mummy found in the back of a truck.

The truth turned into a sinister nightmare. Tests proved the mummy a fake and the body inside it that of a young girl who had been murdered and her internal organs surgically removed. When other identical mummies appeared in other parts of the world Ray had realised that the mummies were the cynical end product of a sick scheme to provide human organs for transplant on the black market. An international manhunt was triggered and the supplier behind the world-wide conspiracy exacted a terrible revenge; an act which ended in the death of the only woman Ray had ever loved.

In the weeks after her death he had shunned friends and family, shutting himself away and drinking himself into a constant state of oblivion in the vain hope that the hurt would go away. In the darkness of his alcohol fuelled existence he kept asking himself the question that is so familiar to those who treat survivors of major disasters: 'Why couldn't it have been me?'

The move to the North therefore represented a new start; a clean break; a chance to start over in a place where nobody knew his past; where nobody knew the baggage he was carrying.

And then Kylie Morris was murdered .

When Bob Craymer told Tracey Morris that he lived "out Heaton way" she had assumed that he lived in the modest suburb. However, the house outside which Detective Constables Paul Prendergast and Mark Blake found themselves — the address they had obtained from Craymer's employer, Bradford City Council — was elsewhere. True, it could be loosely described as "out Heaton way" but it was, in fact, in the adjacent neighbourhood of Manningham, a predominantly Asian area characterised by its serried ranks of solid, stone terraces, built to house the city's once-burgeoning population of textile workers. Many of the current residents had spent a great deal of time and money on their homes, installing new bathrooms, new kitchens, central heating, double glazing and modern, faux-Regency doors in white PVC, complete with deadlocks, that leant an air of incongruity to the squat, Victorian properties.

But the door upon which Prendergast and Blake knocked managed to look out of place even there. It may once have been blue, but its paint work was so faded, its cracks and chips retouched with so many shades of primer, it was difficult to be certain. The bottom of the door was showing signs of rot, mirroring the single sash window to its left. There was no knocker and a cheap plastic bell push hung helplessly from a single strand of wire, signposting its uselessness.

Prendergast sighed, hammered on the door with his fist and stood back, awaiting the nauseating aroma he knew would accompany its opening. It would be a mix of human body odour, burnt fat, boiled cabbage and general accumulated grime. When the door was finally dragged open, the unmistakable redolence of neglect was crowned by something else — the pungent stench that only comes from a collection of cats. Both men involuntarily rocked backwards as the stink hit them.

The man who held the door ajar was around six feet tall with cropped hair and a well-toned torso, shown off by a closely fitting white singlet. He wore jogging bottoms and was bare footed. 'What?' he barked, ignoring the warrant cards that both men held at arm's length in front of them.

'Are you Robert Craymer?' asked Prendergast.

'Who's asking?' he said, still ignoring the badges of authority.

Even after this brief exchange, Prendergast's patience was wearing thin but professionalism was keeping his annoyance in check.

'Detective Constables Prendergast and Blake. West Yorkshire Police Major Incident Team. We'd like to ask you a few questions about Kylie Morris.'

'Kylie? What about her?' Craymer's bravado was suddenly retreating.

Prendergast knew the conversation could not be continued on the doorstep so, against his better judgement, he asked: 'Mr Craymer, can we go inside?'

Without answering, Craymer turned, walked back into the narrow hallway and pushed open the door to the small living room. As he did so he started clapping his hands to shoo out a number of cats that had been sleeping in there. Blake counted six.

'Have a seat. D'you want a brew?' Craymer asked.

Neither man moved towards the proffered seats, secretly fearing what might be concealed there as they tried not to gag on the stench. Blake spoke for them both when he said: 'No thanks Mr Craymer. We had one a few minutes ago. We've got a lot to get through so if you don't mind...'

As Craymer lowered himself into a well-worn armchair, Prendergast asked: 'When did you last see Kylie Morris?'

'Let me think. That would be Tuesday. At the after-school swimming lesson. What's this about anyway?'

'Mr Craymer, I'm afraid we have some bad news,' Blake responded. 'I'm afraid Kylie's dead. She's been murdered.'

'What? When? How? I mean, why?' Depending on the cynicism of the listener, this was a jumble of emotional reactions that were either perfectly natural or a learned response to cover up a deeper knowledge. And the two policemen were very cynical indeed. In their books, everybody had a guilty secret: all you had to do was find it.

'I knew she was missing of course. I saw it on the telly. But dead. You don't expect that. How's her mother? She's a cracker is Tracey.'

The detectives exchanged a glance which Craymer totally misinterpreted.

'You've not seen her? You don't know what you're missing. No spring chicken but a cracking body and...'

Before he got the chance to embroider his description, Prendergast jumped in.

'Mr Craymer, we're here to talk about Kylie so can we please stick to the subject? I understand you rang her mother to ask where she was. Why did you do that?'

Craymer's brow furrowed slightly, as if he was trying to recall the incident.

'Oh yeah. That was Thursday, about teatime,' he remembered. 'Kylie hadn't shown up for her swimming lesson — she goes Tuesday and Thursday every week, never misses — and I was worried she might be ill or something.'

'You're a swimming teacher?' asked Blake.

'Yes. I work at the pool.'

'And how many kids do you get turning up?'

'It varies. Usually about 20, but sometimes more.'

'So why would the health of one individual little girl be of concern to you?'

'Because Kylie's special.'

'How do you mean, *special*?' It was Prendergast's turn.

'She's —was — a really talented swimmer. I expected her to be picked for the junior county swimming team this year and, with the right coaching; she could have gone on to swim for Great Britain in a few years. It wasn't like her to miss out on a lesson.'

'So what was her mother's reaction when you rang to ask if she was OK?'

'Well, like you'd imagine, Tracey was very worried and extremely upset. I suggested she call a few of Kylie's friends to see if she was there and I promised to ring her if she showed up late at the pool.'

Blake decided it was time to play Bad Cop. 'Mr Craymer, twice in the last few minutes you have referred to Mrs Morris by her first name. Do you know the first name of all your pupils' mothers?'

'Er, no.'

'Then why is it you're so familiar with Mrs Morris?'

'Like I just told you. Kylie was an extremely talented swimmer. I was giving her extra coaching on a Saturday morning. Her mum used to bring her and we got talking. Like you do.'

Bad Cop Blake pressed harder. 'You were supposed to be coaching Kylie to become a swimming superstar, not chatting up her mother.'

'I wasn't chatting her up I...'

'I'm getting the impression you were more interested in Mrs Morris than you were in her daughter.'

'It wasn't like that...'

'No? What was it like then Mr Craymer.'

'Tracey — Mrs Morris — started asking me all sorts of questions about Kylie's prospects. You know, what were the next steps? How much would it cost? All that kind of stuff. So we began going for coffee, the three of us, after swimming, so we could discuss it properly.'

'And how often did this happen?'

'Every week. There was always something she wanted to know.'

'And what advice were you able to impart from your vast reservoir of knowledge?'

'Well I told her not to worry about cost because I said I'd coach her for free and explained that when she started competing at a high level, she could get grants to help with travel and stuff.'

Like a terrier on the hunt Blake had picked up a scent and wasn't going to let go.

'Isn't that cosy?' he said. 'Your star pupil happens to have a good looking mother — "cracking" I think is the description you used — who is anxious about her daughter's potential and therefore attentive to the words of the man she thinks can make her dreams come true. So you all troop off to the cafe to play happy families. Not just once, but every week. Come off it Craymer. Tell me the truth about your relationship with Tracey Morris.'

Craymer's cheeks had flushed but whether it was through anger or embarrassment, neither detective could tell.

'No. You've got it all wrong. There was no relationship. She's happily married.'

'And you Mr Craymer. Are you married?' asked Prendergast, knowing the answer before it came.

'Not any more. I was, but we got divorced. That's how I ended up here in this shithole.'

Yeah, thought Blake, and I bet surrounding yourself with stinking cats is the closest you get to pussy too.

Prendergast had opened his wallet and was proffering Craymer a business card. 'If you think of anything else, you can get me on either of those numbers,' he said, suddenly terminating the interview. 'Thanks for your help.'

The first few minutes of the drive back to the police station passed in silence, a silence that was broken by Prendergast. 'So, what do you think of our Mr Craymer then?'

'I think he knows more than he's letting on. He's hiding something,' answered Blake, still in Bad Cop mode.

'I think you might be right but I'm not sure it has anything to do with our inquiry. That said, I think we should keep him on the Persons of Interest file.'

'Oh, he's certainly that,' said Blake. 'And I suspect he'll turn out to be of greater interest than either of us knows right now.'

About the same time, on the opposite side of the city, Ray Wilson and Jan Holroyd were knocking on the door of a small, semi-detached house diametrically opposed to the one Prendergast and Blake had just left. This one had a tiny but well-cared for front garden; its paintwork had that freshly applied look and its windows gleamed.

Jan had taken the call just as she and her boss were leaving the pub they had been to for lunch where, far from being chatty and revealing something of his past career as she had hoped, Ray had been quiet and reflective, saying next to nothing. He had been content to listen, albeit distractedly, as Jan had done all the talking. The call signalled a potential breakthrough in the investigation.

'We've got a witness who says she saw Kylie Morris getting into a van,' she told Ray and gave him an address, slipping the mobile back into her pocket.

The door was opened by a woman in her late 30s whose face wore a troubled expression. Inside, the comfortably furnished living room was dominated by a gigantic 50 inch plasma screen television fixed to the wall above the fireplace. A small bookcase was filled with paperbacks — celebrity autobiographies, love stories and a few cookery books. No prizes for guessing who does the reading in this house, thought Ray.

'It's my daughter Madison. She's in the same class as Kylie Morris,' began Sheena Foxcroft. 'They weren't mates or anything but obviously they knew each other. Well, the thing is, she only told me this just now; otherwise I'd have called earlier...'

Jan interrupted. 'Mrs Foxcroft there's nothing to worry about. You've done exactly the right thing. Can we speak to Madison?'

'Oh. Yes. Of course. I'll get her.'

Less than a minute later she returned with the terrified looking 12 year-old, her hair held back in a ponytail. She twisted her fingers around themselves as if she was searching for a secure grip to stop herself falling.

It was Jan who took the lead. 'Hello Madison. I expect Mum's told you we're police officers but there's absolutely nothing to worry about. We just want to ask you some questions about Kylie. Kylie Morris? I believe you knew her.'

A voice so soft as to be almost inaudible answered, 'Yes. We were in the same class.'

'And did you see her last Thursday?'

'I saw her at school, yes.'

'Did you see her after school at all?'

The little girl's face creased and tears welled in her eyes.

'Madison, you know, don't you, that something terrible has happened to Kylie?' asked Ray. An indiscernible nod. 'Well, it's our job to catch whoever did those awful things to Kylie and we think you can help us. So it's very important that you tell us everything you know; everything you saw. Is that OK?'

Another slight nod.

'OK then, why don't you tell us in your own words what you saw. Take your time.'

Madison regained her composure. 'It was Thursday. Kylie always goes swimming on Tuesdays and Thursdays after school. She's always going swimming. Usually she gets the school bus because it goes near the swimming pool but on Thursday she didn't.'

'How do you know that Madison,' asked Jan.

'Because I saw her getting in a van.'

'Go on,' encouraged Jan. 'Tell us where you saw this.'

'It was round the corner from school, in Mayfield Avenue. It's on my way home. Kylie was walking. She was quite a bit in front of me.'

Ray interrupted again. 'How can you be sure it was Kylie?'

'Because of her red hair. No one else in our class has hair like that.'

'OK Madison, you're doing very well. Carry on,' said Jan.

'Well, there was a van parked at the side of the road. I saw her stop and talk to the driver. Then she went round and got in the passenger side.'

'Madison, this is very, very important information. Well done,' Ray said. 'Can you tell us anything about the van? Do you know what make it was? What colour it was?'

'It was a red one but I don't know what sort it was.'

'It were a Transit. A Ford Transit Connect.' The Yorkshire accent heavy and unmistakable.

The four pair of eyes in the room swivelled simultaneously in the direction of the doorway, where the voice had come from.

Leaning on the door jamb was a boy a couple of years older than Madison, wearing a grey hooded sweater, baggy black track suit trousers with elasticated ankles and huge trainers that appeared too large for his feet. The uniform of youth.

'How long have you been there?' started Sheena Foxcroft, then, turning to the police officers explained, 'This is Bradley. Madison's brother. My eldest.'

'Bradley, do come and join us,' Ray said. 'Tell us how you can be so sure about the make of the van.'

'Everybody knows what a Transit Connect looks like. Besides, my mate's Dad's got one. He's a plumber. Says it's the best van he's ever had.'

'Did you see Kylie getting into it?'

'Yeah. I thought it was her Dad or something.'

'Why didn't you come forward when we appealed for help?' asked Ray.

'Didn't know anything about it did I? Just heard you lot talking. First I knew about it.'

'Alright Bradley. Where were you when you saw Kylie?'

'I was on the school bus, driving past.'

'You weren't with your sister? You weren't walking home with her?'

'No chance. I got street cred to protect man.'

'I don't suppose you got the registration number did you?'

'Get real man.'

Bradford's new police headquarters sat in the heart of an area of light industrial buildings about half a mile from the city centre, its 'reconstituted' stone finish at odds with its surroundings, which were either soot-blackened millstone grit or 1960s brick and cladding. But it was easy to get in and out of and there was ample parking, a fact that caused more than one retired officer to ponder how far policing had come since the days when police stations were built in the heart of the communities they looked after.

Ray and Jan arrived back around the same time as Prendergast and Blake. The four of them were in Ray's office discussing developments over canteen coffee. 'So what makes you think Mr Craymer is not being particularly forthcoming?' asked Ray.

'It's nothing specific,' replied Prendergast. 'It's just that we've both got the feeling that he knows more than he's letting on but at this stage I can't imagine what it might be. If that makes sense.'

Blake added: 'He seems to know a lot more about Kylie's mum than he does about her, even though he's supposed to be her swimming coach. I think it was the way he kept referring to her by her first name. I reckon he was coaching her for something else, if you know what I mean.'

'Just because he wants to shag somebody doesn't make him a killer,' said Jan. 'Christ, if that were true most of the men in Britain would be behind bars.'

'I think we should keep our Mr Craymer as being of significant interest but the best lead we've got right now is the sighting — by two of her fellow pupils — of Kylie getting into a red Ford Transit Connect around the corner from school,' said Ray. 'We need to trawl all the CCTV footage we can find from the area and see if we can track it.'

'Do you want us to issue a statement through the Press Office,' asked Jan. 'Y'know, asking for anybody who might have seen it in the area, that sort of stuff.'

Ray pondered for a minute. 'No, I don't think so. Not at this stage. If we alert whoever was driving it too soon we just give him more time to get rid of it and destroy whatever evidence there might be inside it. No. For now, we don't make anything public about the van.'

CHAPTER 9

It had been two weeks since Kylie Morris had been found, clinging to life by the slenderest of threads, a thread which was to prove insufficiently strong to hold her in this world. Two weeks in which Ray Wilson and his team had made absolutely no progress in their hunt for whoever was responsible for mercilessly beating the 12 year-old and dumping her, naked, like a sack of refuse, on a lonely road. Two weeks in which team morale had slumped. They needed a break.

The team's office was dominated by a huge white board, at the centre of which was a photograph of Kylie. Around it was every bit of information that had been gathered; some of it linked by hand-drawn lines, and included pictures of the spot where Kylie's body had been found. There was also a picture of Bob Craymer and the swimming pool where he worked. Some information that had been checked and found to be worthless had been erased, leaving behind splodges of felt-tip pen. There was also a list of things still be done. It was a very short list.

The one lead they had — the red Ford Transit Connect which two witnesses had seen Kylie climb into of her own free will — had so far drawn a blank. The team, augmented by a few uniforms dragged in for the purpose, had trawled through hours of CCTV footage covering every possible route away from the school. More than a dozen red Ford Transit Connects had been identified, their owners and drivers quizzed. One had been subjected to a thorough forensic examination. But none had yielded a clue to Kylie Morris. The vehicle she had got into had simply vanished, indicating that the driver either had an intimate knowledge of the city's CCTV network, or that he was one lucky guy.

Ray was in his glass-walled office, a structure that made him feel like a sea creature in an aquarium, contemplating playing the only card he was holding and releasing the information they had on the van when Jan Holroyd, dispensing with the formalities of a knock, stuck her head round the door. 'Forensics have come up with something, guv,' she said.

There was no reaction from her DCI, not that she really expected one, other than the obvious. 'Is it any use?'

'It might be,' replied Jan. 'They've found hairs on the duct tape that was wrapped round the girl's mouth. Cat hairs.'

'Cat hairs? Great. Don't tell me. We're looking for a six foot moggy with paws the size of hams and a driving licence.'

'Now, now,' she chided, only half-jokingly. 'It could be important. The lab says the hairs appear to be from more than one cat but that they could match them to individual animals. They just need other samples. So they can do a DNA match.'

Ray threw his pen down on his desk. 'Now you're pulling my pisser Holroyd. A DNA match? On a cat?'

'Apparently so,' said Jan. 'According to the lab guys, the Yanks have already got a cat DNA database and a bloke in Canada has been convicted of second-degree murder using cat hair DNA to link him to the crime. Don't ask me how it works. They did try to explain but I didn't understand a word. That's why they wear white coats and I carry handcuffs. The one thing that did tickle me though is the name of the DNA test. It's called "Meowplex".'

'You're being serious aren't you?' Ray said. 'But I don't see how cat DNA can be of help to us.'

'Think back guv. To when Prendergast and Blake went to see Bob Craymer, the guy that first alerted Tracey Morris that Kylie hadn't turned up at swimming.'

'Yeah. So what?'

'Do you remember they said the house smelled like a zoo? Because it was full of cats.'

Jan could almost see the light switch on in Ray's eyes.

'Holroyd, I could kiss you. Get Prendergast and Blake in here now.'

The two detective constables grinned like — Jan could think of no other simile — Cheshire cats as she filled them in on what she learned from the forensic lab. When she'd finished her briefing, Ray carried on. 'This could be the best lead we've got so far,' he said. 'You'll need a search warrant but I want Craymer's place turned over from top to bottom. Take a SOCO with you to gather cat hair for the DNA test and a couple of uniforms to help with the search. We're looking for duct tape,

cable ties and any photographs or paperwork that might link him to a red
Ford Transit Connect, or anything he might have that's Kylie's.'

This time Bob Craymer wasn't nearly as cocky when he opened his
rotting, multi-coloured front door. The stench from inside was
undiminished but faced with the two detectives, four uniformed officers
and two SOCOs, his demeanour was distinctly contrite. Mark Blake
waved the search warrant under his nose. 'Robert Craymer. We have a
warrant to search these premises in connection with the death of Kylie
Morris.'

Craymer could only stammer: 'Am I...am...am I under arrest?'

'Not yet Mr Craymer,' replied Blake. 'But it depends on what we find.'
He pushed past Craymer, pulling a pair of blue latex gloves from his
pocket. To the team that followed behind he said: 'OK, you all know
what to do. Let's get on with it.'

The search of the tiny terraced property took more than three hours,
largely because the searchers kept finding excuses to go outside, just so
they could breathe air that wasn't fetid and poisoned with the stink of
cats. At the end of it, the SOCOs had collected more than two dozen
samples of cat hair from the furniture and carpets as well as samples cut
directly from the back of the six cats which Craymer admitted to owning,
along with samples from stains found on the sofa and an armchair that
faced the giant plasma TV. They also took a DNA sample from Craymer.
The search of the house had revealed Craymer's liking for pornography,
a handful of old swimming trophies forgotten at the back of a cupboard
and his wedding album, the only trace of his former wife that he had not
destroyed. But there was nothing to link him to a van of any make, size
or colour and no trace of Kylie Morris. A roll of duct tape found stuffed
away under the sink initially raised hopes until Blake recognised that it
was the wrong colour.

'Satisfied now?' he yelled at the retreating backs of the detectives, his
bravado beginning to return. 'I keep telling you I know nothing about
what happened to Kylie.'

Back at their vehicle the SOCOs peeled off their white plastic suits and
face masks, revealing two women, both in their early 30s, who all at once
looked remarkably normal. 'I don't know about you guys,' said one of
them, addressing Prendergast and Blake, 'but we're going back to take a

very long, very hot shower. I've been in some shitholes in this job but that one takes the biscuit. It never ceases to amaze me the conditions some people choose to live in.'

'Yeah. Not good is it,' replied Blake. 'Any idea when you'll have something for us?'

The SOCO shook her long blonde hair free from the elastic band that had held it in a tight bun and let it cascade over her shoulders. 'The stains shouldn't take too long,' she said. 'I'm pretty certain what they are right now but we need to compare them to his DNA sample to make sure he's made them. The cat hair could take longer. To be honest we've never done one before. We know what to do, of course, and we know what we're looking for, but it's new ground for us. We'll be in touch as soon as we have a result.'

Prendergast sniffed suspiciously at the sleeve of his suit as the two detectives walked to their car. 'Christ. This is going to have to go to the cleaners,' he said. 'It stinks of fucking cats.' As an aside to his colleague he added, 'And you can put your tongue away now. She's gone.'

'Yeah but she was tasty though wasn't she?' asked Blake. 'She could run tests on me anytime.'

'Bloody hell Blakey, you're woman mad,' joked Prendergast.

'God's gift to mankind mate. There's nothing finer. My old Dad always used to say that if God has made anything finer than a woman he's kept it for himself,' Blake replied. 'Besides, you're only jealous because your hunting days are over now that you've got yourself a little wifey.'

Ray Wilson was well aware that, like the maturation of malt whisky or a fine wine, forensic science was not something that could be rushed. But that didn't stop him anxiously awaiting every post-delivery, or feeling a tiny rush of adrenaline every time the telephone rang. Until the results came through, the enquiry into the murder of Kylie Morris was effectively at a standstill. There were no other leads. The cat hairs were the only key that could potentially open any doors. And the wait was also doing something else; something personal. It was reminding him of the last time he had to wait for forensic scientists to unlock a mystery for him — and of how the results they had revealed ultimately lead to the death of his lover. He tried to push it to the back of his mind but it kept barging its way back to the front, bringing with it a thought too terrible to contemplate: 'What if it happens again?'

He was struggling to suppress an up-welling of these thoughts when Mark Blake tapped on his glass door, opened it and held out a large manila envelope. 'Forensics guv,' he said. 'The lab's just sent them over by courier.'

A look that could have been interpreted as relief crossed Ray's face. 'Great. Thanks Mark. Team briefing in 15 minutes. Can you get it organised?'

'Will do guv.'

As the door closed, Ray wriggled his finger into the top of the envelope and ripped it open, focussing only on its contents. Inside was a summary of the results of the forensic tests and a detailed breakdown of the test results for each individual sample collected by the SOCOs. Ray read through the papers twice then went out to brief his team.

Even though none of the small squad assigned to the investigation of Kylie Morris's murder had more than a passing acquaintance with Ray Wilson, each and every one of them recognised that he was not a happy man as he began his briefing on the forensic findings. If his office door had been an old fashioned wooden one, it would have slammed with a noise like thunder. Instead, the soft-close hinges allowed it to close gently and quietly, absorbing the fury and the force with which it was thrown shut.

Ray threw the torn manila envelope and its contents on a desk. 'Right,' he barked uncharacteristically. 'As I'm sure you all know by now, the forensics are back. And a fat lot of fucking good they are too.

'First, the bad news. The stains found on the sofa and the armchair are semen. Craymer's semen. I'm not going to speculate how they got there but you can bet a year's pay they weren't the result of a passionate hands-on encounter with a Scandinavian blonde of Amazonian proportions.

'Now, more bad news. The DNA matches on the cat hairs found on the duct tape and the samples taken from Craymer's menagerie are all negative. The hairs on the duct tape did not come from Craymer's cats.

'I'm reasonably confident that Kylie Morris was never in that house which means people, we're back to square one. We've got nothing solid. The only thing we've got is the sighting of Kylie getting into a red Ford

Transit which, as you are aware, we've kept to ourselves until now. Now we don't have a choice, we have to release that information and appeal for anyone else who may have seen Kylie getting into the van. Or anyone who may have seen her in the van on the road. Or anybody who knows some bugger who owned a red Ford Transit Connect three weeks ago and now doesn't.

'Jan, can I leave it to you to liaise with the Press Office? You know what to say. Just don't make it look like we're clutching at straws.

'And while we're at it, I want a thorough search done of every scrap yard within a 10 mile radius to see if anybody has scrapped a red Transit Connect recently. I know it's a ball-acher and it's a needle-in-a-haystack job but it has to be done. Carve it up between yourselves. And if a 10 mile radius doesn't find anything we'll go to 20 miles and then 30 and 40 and 50 if we have to. That van's out there somewhere and we need to find it.'

Ray marched back to his glass-box office and slumped in his imitation leather executive chair, lost in his thoughts and not even bothering to close the door. He swung the chair to face the window and its view over the public transport interchange to the city's town hall. Beyond it, on the horizon, he could just make out the streets of Manningham where Craymer lived and where, he was convinced, the clues to Kylie's killer lay. Try as he may, he couldn't stop pondering the circumstances that had brought him to this tough, uncompromising, neglected, yet strangely attractive area of Britain.

He'd been offered counselling, of course, but had rejected it, seeing it as a sign of weakness. He had to deal with what had happened in his own way. Nothing would bring Karen back and nothing would take away the self-doubt that had dogged him since that fateful day. Everything came back to the question 'What if?' What if he'd followed his orders to the letter? What if he'd kept his relationship with Karen strictly professional? What if he'd not let her panic him into going on the run with her?

In the end he decided to turn his back on everything he'd ever known and start afresh. He'd looked at jobs in police forces all over Britain. He'd even thought of asking for a transfer to Interpol headquarters in Lyon. Giving up police work altogether and doing something proper with his history of art degree had crossed his mind. Then he saw the West

Yorkshire job advertised — and it had crooked an inviting finger to him as if saying: 'This is where you belong.'

'Penny for 'em guv.' The voice of Jan Holroyd dragged him back to reality.

'Come in Jan. What can I do for you?' he said.

'I just thought I'd let you know that I've spoken to the Press Office,' Jan said. 'They'll issue a statement about the Transit but, like they said, interest in Kylie's murder seems to have waned. Even the Telegraph & Argus haven't run anything on it for ages.'

'Yes, I'm aware of that but we have to hope it will revive some interest.' He sensed that Jan hadn't just popped in to give him a progress report. 'Anything else?'

'Er, not really. It's just...' she was debating whether to continue. 'It's just that trawling round scrap yards is going to be massive job, especially for such a small team. And there's probably an easier way to do it. Like, every vehicle that's scrapped has to be reported to DVLA so it'll be on their database so we could short-circuit things by...' She got no further.

'Sergeant Holroyd,' he said sharply, 'I don't need you or anybody else to tell me how to short-circuit things. That's how things get missed. Modern technology isn't infallible. It can be cheated. It can be manipulated. It can be just wrong. So if I say I want every fucking scrap yard in the country turned over with a fine tooth comb that's exactly what will happen. Do you understand?'

'Er, yes sir. Perfectly sir.'

'Good. Now get on with it. And close the door behind you.'

As the door swished shut, he was stabbed by a bitter pang of regret. Shouting at his team like an arsehole wouldn't bring Karen back either.

CHAPTER 10

Ray was close to despair. The media appeal had produced precisely nothing. Yes, it had briefly revived interest in the murder of Kylie Morris. Yes, the story had made the front page of the Bradford Telegraph & Argus and he had patiently conducted interviews with the two regional television stations and three local radio stations. But the net result was a big fat zero. The trawl of scrap yards was going on as he'd instructed but that too had revealed nothing of interest so far.

The self-doubt was becoming stronger. This was his first big job in his new rank in his new force. He couldn't fail. And yet the enquiry was going nowhere and he knew the team's morale was sinking by the day. He'd read and re-read every document, every note, every report that had been written about Kylie's death. He'd even started taking them home — against force standing orders — in the forlorn hope that in the comfort of his moorland cottage, glass of single malt in hand, a spark of inspiration might lighten the darkness. But the lamp remained unlit.

And then the telephone rang.

In another state of mind, Ray might well have told the caller to piss off and stop wasting his time. But he was a man desperate to prove his worth to his bosses, his colleagues, his team and, most of all, to the memory of his beloved Karen. So when the caller told him that he was a child psychologist and that he had a young patient who was having nightmares that could possibly have a bearing on his inquiry, Ray sat up and took notice.

'I think it's only fair to tell you that I have serious concerns about the wisdom of making this call,' Dr Stephen Parke told him. 'First of all, I believe it could be ethically dubious — there's the whole question of patient confidentiality for a start — but the little girl's parents have given me permission to contact you because they believe, rightly or wrongly, that if you catch your murderer their daughter's problems will cease.

'And then, more importantly, there is the issue of how exposing this little girl to a police investigation will affect her mentally.'

Ray, desperately reaching out like a drowning man grasping for a lifebelt, said reassuringly: 'I don't think you've got anything to worry about on that score Dr Parke. We have vast experience of dealing with vulnerable witnesses. But I think we need to meet so we can discuss the details before we progress.'

'I think that's a very good idea Chief Inspector,' Parke replied. 'I can't take the risk of damaging Samantha any more than she already has been so we need to proceed with great caution. My colleague and I are available tomorrow afternoon, if that's convenient.'

He was content for Jan Holroyd to drive on the 45 minute journey over the Pennines to Manchester while he pondered the sketchy information that Dr Stephen Parke had given him. Incredible as it sounded, it was enough to give him hope. But Jan was highly sceptical — and let him know it.

'Boss, don't take this personally,' she said as their car joined the motorway, 'but I can't help thinking this is going to be a dead end. No pun intended.'

'What do you mean?'

'Well, what possible bearing could a kid having nightmares in Manchester have on the murder of another kid in Bradford? You have to admit it sounds unlikely.'

'I'm admitting nothing of the kind until we've heard what Dr Parke and his chum have to say. And I would expect my senior DS to keep an open mind too. Let's not go in there with preconceived notions.'

'Yeah, OK boss,' said Jan. 'It's just that...'

'Just what?' snapped Ray.

Jan decided to keep her thoughts to herself. 'Nothing boss. Nothing.'

Her scepticism, however, was not diminished on meeting Stephen Parke and his colleague Richard Fairfax. Parke's secretary had offered them her usual invitation to tea — 'Earl Grey or builder's?' — and the psychologist began by describing the ethical dilemma he and his colleague were under in that both of them believed their young patient was witnessing, in her ever more violent nightmares, the death of another child, but that patient confidentiality should preclude them from talking about it. However, in this instance, the girl's parents were so desperate for a resolution to their daughter's problems that they had authorised the doctors to reveal everything to the police in the hope that if the information helped solve the crime, the nightmares would end.

Fairfax had begun by trying to explain the theory of cellular memory. Trendy fucking medics, Jan had decided after the first five minutes. He gave them a PowerPoint presentation which did nothing to alter Jan's perceptions but which did include references to all the research done into the theory in America and the anecdotal evidence to support it.

Ray listened intently, but as far as Jan was concerned it was nothing more than cranky Yankee pseudo-science and would contribute zilch to their hunt for Kylie's killer. She let her mind wander, not taking particular notice of Fairfax's voice as he described in great detail the nightmares that had plagued Samantha Lowe. He described how they had first struggled to interpret the box-like drawings she had made and the coloured flashes that went with them; how she had spoken of a man she feared was going to hit her with an object he held in his hand and how things had begun to fall into place after he had read the appeal in the Daily Telegraph for information relating to a red Ford Transit Connect. Even when Fairfax mentioned the date on which Samantha Lowe had undergone her heart transplant operation — the day on which Kylie's life support had been switched off — the significance didn't register with Jan.

Even when he followed that up with, 'And we have unofficial confirmation that the heart she was given came from your murder victim,' she still did not give him her undivided attention.

Ray, on the other hand, was becoming more and more animated. He was hanging on the doctors' every word, absorbing everything they said, mentally attempting to compartmentalise it into the framework of his murder enquiry. Improbable as it seemed, this could be his lifeline; the only bit of good news he'd had in the investigation of the murder of Kylie Morris; a heaven-sent opportunity to catch her killer. And it was an opportunity he wasn't going to let slip. When Parke and Fairfax had finished all they had to say, Ray said bluntly, 'Right. Sounds like we're on to something here. I want to speak to this Samantha girl myself.'

The medics threw each other nervous glances, looks of apprehension that did not escape Ray. 'What's the matter? Is there a problem with that?' he asked.

It was Parke who answered first. 'Mr Wilson, you must understand that Samantha Lowe is still only seven years old. She's still suffering these terribly distressing nightmares and mentally she's highly vulnerable. I cannot take the risk of exposing her to a police interrogation. It could do untold harm.'

'Dr Parke, I have no intention of interrogating her, as you put it,' said Ray. 'But it's vital that I hear for myself what this little girl has to say. I have to tell you that your theory that the murdered girl's memory lives on in her transplanted heart is incredible to say the least. But what you've told me does appear to have at least a tangential connection with the path of our enquiry. That's why it is absolutely essential that I speak to Samantha personally. You can relay every dot and comma of what she's said to you but evidentially, it's still hearsay. So gentlemen, if you can't find some way of letting me speak to her, I'm afraid this has all been a waste of time.'

He stood to leave, his frustration barely concealed. 'We need some time to discuss this between ourselves and with Samantha's parents,' said Parke. 'There may be a way in which we can allow you to witness her talking about her experiences but we would need to get back to you.'

'Very well, I'll wait to hear from you,' said Ray. 'Just bear in mind the nature of this enquiry.'

For the first 15 minutes of the return journey, Jan Holroyd didn't say a word. Ray was pretending to stare distractedly out of the passenger window when he suddenly said: 'OK Sergeant Holroyd. Out with it. What're you thinking?'

'Thinking? Nothing guv. I don't know what you mean,' she stumbled.

'Yes you do Holroyd,' said Ray. 'You think that what we've just heard is a load of old bollocks. That it's too far-fetched to be true and that even if it was true, it would never stand up in court — that is if the CPS ever stopped laughing long enough to present it. But I have to tell you that from where I'm sitting, it's the best — the only — lead we've got right now so I've got to run with it. Now, feel free to shoot me down if you want to.'

Jan glanced across at her boss, not fully understanding why he had suddenly become, as she saw it, a vociferous convert to a theory that had no place outside the realms of science fiction.

'No guv, don't get me wrong,' she started. 'I don't want to shoot you down. It's just that, well, you know what they say about things that seem too good to be true — they usually are. I know how badly you want a result on this one but I'm worried that you're about to put all your eggs in one basket.'

'Make that egg singular, Sergeant,' Ray said. 'I am about to put my egg in one basket and I am very aware that it's a basket with a lot of holes in it. But it's the only basket I've got.'

'Yeah, alright guv. I can't say that I totally believe all that shite about memory not just being in the brain but you can count on my full support. I want this bastard as much as you do.'

Four days went by before Stephen Parke called again. After a brief exchange of pleasantries he got down to the reason for his call. To Ray Wilson he sounded like a man with his back to the wall. 'Mr Wilson, we've discussed your request to speak to Samantha with her parents,' he said. 'We explained your position fully and they understand that their daughter may be the only positive lead in your enquiry. However, we also explained our position, which is that everything we do must be in Samantha's best interests. We told them that we had already refused your request and that we thought it only fair to tell them so. They agreed with that decision.'

Ray, who was running out of patience as well as ideas, interrupted him. 'Yeah, well, thanks doc. Sorry to have wasted both our time...'

He was about to drop the telephone back on its cradle when Parke added hurriedly, 'But they have agreed to a compromise.'

'A compromise? What kind of compromise?' Ray asked.

'Well, we have a couple of counselling suites here at the hospital that are equipped with CCTV,' said Park. 'Mr and Mrs Lowe have agreed to let Richard and I talk to Samantha in one of those suites while you watch a relay. Then you could take away a DVD to study at your leisure. I know it's not perfect but it's the best you're going to get I'm afraid.'

Ray thought for a second. 'Would you be able to ask Samantha questions I give you beforehand?'

'I don't see why not, as long as they don't cause her unnecessary distress.'

After he'd put the 'phone down, Ray sat staring blankly at the glass wall of his office. He still wasn't going to get to talk to Samantha himself, but getting someone else to ask the questions was the best he was going to get. It was probably going to be his only opportunity to test Richard Fairfax's incredible theory. He had to take it, no matter how sceptical he was of a result. He didn't have a choice. He would accept the invitation. But he would frame some very careful questions. 'Holroyd,' he yelled at his open door. 'I need your help. Now.'

The questions the two of them had put together had been e-mailed to Stephen Parke the day before the scheduled interview date. The list sought answers that Ray believed were vital to solving Kylie's murder and included: Did the van take you to another place? Do you know where it was? Can you describe anything about the place? Can you see the face of the man who is going to hit you? Can you describe him for us? Does he say anything to you? What does he say? Does he know your name? Does he hit you while you're in the van?

Now, Ray and Jan sat together on a bright green sofa in a windowless room in the shiny, new Royal Manchester Children's Hospital. On the wall, a flat-screen television monitor was showing an empty bean-bag — in the same colour of green — in another room somewhere else in the hospital. For what seemed like hours, the picture didn't change but then, suddenly, just as Ray was about to announce his boredom, the bean-bag was occupied by a little girl. She was wearing a pink designer track-suit and white leather trainers. Her blonde hair was swept back off her face, held by an Alice band across the top of her forehead. Ray was immediately struck by how frail she looked; how careworn; as if she carried the weight of the world on her young shoulders. Then he heard Stephen Parke's familiar, measured tones as he began to speak to Samantha Lowe.

The interview lasted more than hour with Parke and Fairfax each asking questions, gently probing, going over ground they had covered with Samantha time and time again. The answers they received, the information they were given, was unchanged. And there was nothing new. Because they hadn't asked a single question put forward by Ray and Jan.

The screen went to black as the interview ended. As it did so, Ray exploded, almost drowning out the disembodied voice of Dr Parke as it floated from a pair of hidden speakers. 'DCI Wilson, please stay where you are. We'll be with you very shortly.'

By the time the two medics appeared, Ray had calmed down a little. But not much. Before either of them spoke, Ray jumped in. 'If you don't mind me asking *doctors*,' he spat, 'what the fuck was that? You didn't ask one question that we wanted answering. You didn't elicit one bit of information that we didn't already know. You didn't do anything to help my enquiry one bit. As far as I'm concerned it's been a total waste of time.'

'Mr Wilson,' Parke began, 'you ought to know that...' He didn't get any further.

'Why the hell did you ask me to submit questions if you weren't going to ask them?' yelled Ray.

'You saw Samantha. She's an extremely vulnerable child. We didn't think it was appropriate...' Again, an angry Ray leapt in.

'Appropriate? Appropriate? We're trying to catch an extremely cruel and violent killer here. Nothing that can help us in that aim can be deemed "not appropriate".'

Parke made a gesture that could have been an indication of resignation or a sign of frustration. 'Mr Wilson, Richard and I discussed your questions at great length last night. I'm sorry we didn't have chance to explain to you before we started but we felt that some of the questions you put forward would be exceptionally distressing for Samantha, forcing her to confront things that she may have subconsciously buried.'

'But the whole point is that she may have information that is vital to tracking down the killer of Kylie Morris,' said Ray. 'If Samantha gets upset by recalling it, she'll get over it. If it takes the enquiry forward one inch I'd say that was a fair exchange.'

'No Mr Wilson. You don't seem to understand the gravity of the situation,' said Parke. 'I'm not talking about Samantha being upset for an hour or two. I'm talking about her being psychologically damaged for the rest of her life.'

'That's bullshit and you know it,' Ray said. 'You're forcing me down a road I don't want to go down. I may have to consider taking action to force you to ask those questions.'

'You can take whatever action you like Mr Wilson. But I will always act in the best interests of my patient.'

'I've heard enough of this crap. Holroyd, come on. I need a drink.'

It was still before 11.00am so Jan Holroyd steered her irate boss towards the hospital cafe.

As soon as they stepped through the door they saw her. A little girl dressed in a pink designer track suit, white leather trainers on her feet and her blonde hair swept back, sitting at a table in the centre of the cafe, sipping from a can of Coca Cola through a straw. A man and a woman sat on either side of her.

But Ray saw more.

He stared fixedly at the woman. He saw a slightly built woman in her mid-30s. He saw a pretty, almost elfin-like face with big, clear eyes made bigger by black make up. He saw shoulder length hair, somewhere between blonde and brown, fashionably cut. He saw clear, flawless skin and for a millisecond his fingers tingled at the remembered sensation of caressing it. He saw a women he had loved but who, he believed, he had ultimately let down.

He saw his beloved Karen.

'Boss. Boss. It's them.' Jan's voice and a dig in the ribs from her elbow brought him back. 'Shall we go and talk to them?'

'No. Let's not rush into anything.' Ray's mind was tumbling; thoughts, memories, regrets all falling over each other as he struggled to assimilate what he was seeing. 'Let's get a coffee.'

They sat down with their cappuccinos at a table just one away from the Lowes, but Ray was elsewhere. He was back on his cruiser on the Norfolk Broads with Karen, although in the picture he could see she was bound hand and foot and a man he hated was holding a gun to her head. Yet even with that image in his head he stared and stared, unseeing, at the woman two tables away.

'Boss, they're getting ready to go. We've got to move now,' Jan said insistently.

'What? Oh, yeah. Right.'

Ray stood, taking his warrant card from his jacket pocket as he did so.

'Mr and Mrs Lowe?' More of a statement than a question. 'Sorry to bother you but I'm Detective Chief Inspector Ray Wilson and this is my colleague Detective Sergeant Holroyd. We're from the West Yorkshire Police Major Incident Team. Can we have a word?'

Peter Lowe immediately went on the defensive.

'What about? We can't help you with anything. You'll have to speak to Doctor Parke.'

'Mr Lowe, I understand your concerns. I don't know how much Dr Parke has told you but we are investigating the brutal murder of a young girl and we believe there is a possibility it could be linked to Samantha's problems. We've just witnessed the interview she had with Dr Parke and Dr Fairfax but there are still things we need to know. We really need your help.' The quiet gentility of Ray's approach surprised Jan, revealing a side of his nature she did not believe existed.

'I know all that — that's why we're here. To help,' said Peter. 'We've done what we were asked. I don't see what more we can do. You will have to speak to Dr Parke.'

'The thing is Mr Lowe, you may have done what you were asked, but the good doctors Parke and Fairfax didn't.' The change in Ray's tone was noticeable. 'What we've just sat through was of absolutely no value whatsoever to our enquiry because the doctors took it upon themselves not to ask the questions we wanted answering. So I need to speak to Samantha myself. Directly. Not through a video-link or via a third party. Just me and her. And my sergeant here.'

Jan could sense the frustration rising in her boss and placed a hand on his arm, a gesture, albeit a small one, of restraint. He shrugged her off.

Kate Lowe sat wide-eyed and speechless trying to figure out what had caused such a rapid change in attitude in a man who was a total stranger. Her husband had no time for such thoughts and reacted in a like manner. 'No chance. You know that the doctors won't allow that,' he said. 'We've done the best we can by coming here today. It's not our fault the doctors didn't ask the right questions for you but I can't — I won't — allow you to speak to Samantha unless they say it's OK. Do you understand?'

Before Ray could answer, Peter stood and spoke to his wife and daughter. 'Come on. We're going home now. We've finished what we came to do.'

Ray held Peter's gaze as he prised a card from his jacket pocket and skimmed it across the cafeteria table towards Kate. 'If you change your mind, that's my direct line and my mobile number. Call me.'

As the family walked away Ray called after them: 'And while you're making your mind up, just remember there's a maniac out there who raped a young girl, battered her with a lump of wood and then dumped her over a wall like a sack of rubbish.'

Later Jan would recall that the silence that fell on the busy cafeteria was complete. It was the silence of shock; of other peoples' embarrassment.

CHAPTER 11

The house, he guessed, dated from the late 1940s or early 1950s. Semi-detached, it was solidly built in brick with a slate roof, decent sized, well-tended garden and a short drive that ended in a garage, also built in brick, that shielded the back of the property from prying eyes.

It was one of hundreds of identical houses, made individual only by the owner's choice of paint colour and the layout of the garden, in this part of suburban Cheshire. A 'much sought after area' as estate agents' blurbs described it — beyond the technical boundaries of Manchester but within easy reach of the city centre. The perfect place to live for anyone who worked or played — or did both — in the place that liked to call itself England's Second City.

Ray had taken it all in as his Sat Nav guided him to the address. It was a pleasant enough location. If it had problems they were well concealed and, anyway, they wouldn't be the sort of problems that people who lived in the inner city, any inner city, recognised as problems. There was no graffiti, no boarded-up shops, no derelict buildings, no wastelands littered with discarded hypodermics and condoms. This was firmly middle-class England.

He rang the doorbell and stepped back, as if expecting whoever answered it to come out fists swinging. And he stood to one side, on the same side as the handle, so that the person opening the door would have to open it wide to see who was outside. It was a habit he'd developed over the years. There was no logic to it. He just felt comforted by being able to see inside the house; by knowing that the chances of a surprise hiding behind the door were reduced by his view.

The door opened and he saw again the elfin-like face, the hair, the skin. For a moment they took his breath away.

'Good afternoon Mrs Lowe,' he managed. 'You said you wanted to see me.'

'Mr Wilson. Yes. Good of you to come this far. Do come in.'

Inside, the house was exactly as he expected. Parquet flooring in the hall; a hard-wood staircase dog-legged to the right. Ahead he could see a kitchen that appeared newly fitted featuring a trendy central island and tiled flooring. She showed him into a living room simply but tastefully furnished with leather armchairs and a sofa.

Everywhere he looked there were photographs of Samantha.

Samantha on her own. Samantha with her Mummy. Samantha with her Daddy. Samantha in the garden. Samantha on the beach. Samantha in the countryside. Samantha at the zoo.

If there were pictures of anybody else in the room, they were not obvious.

He was not offered tea or coffee, instead Kate Lowe got straight to the point.

'Mr Wilson I asked you to come and see me because I was very disturbed by what you said as we were leaving the hospital,' she said. 'We knew, of course, that the little girl whose heart Samantha was given had died a violent death. The nightmares you know. And what Dr Parke and Dr Fairfax concluded from them.

'To be honest I'd never thought about it except in the way that it affects Samantha. Until you shouted after us. What must that poor girl's parents be going through? Knowing what that man did to their daughter and knowing that he's out there, free. It must be terrible. That's why I called you.'

'It was a very brave decision,' Ray said. 'You've done the right thing.'

'Please, let me explain,' she said. 'I haven't done anything except pick up the phone. I haven't even told my husband I rang you.'

Ray suddenly felt like a ship-wrecked sailor who'd just had his life-jacket popped.

He'd assumed they'd had a sensible discussion and reached the right decision. Now, it turned out, it was nothing more than a mother on a guilt trip because she hadn't appreciated how distressing it was to have your only daughter kidnapped, raped and murdered.

Rising to his feet he said, 'Look, if you just want to say sorry you could have done that on the phone...'

'No. Mr Wilson please hear me out,' Kate replied. 'I suppose I could have done this on the phone but I thought it would be easier for me face-to-face. I want to help you. I've been thinking about it a lot and I've decided that we should let you speak to Samantha. All I've got to do now is convince Peter that it's a good idea.'

As she spoke, Ray sat mesmerised, watching the movement of her lips as they formed the words, feeling once again their softness on his mouth. It was only when they stopped moving he realised she awaited some kind of response.

He said, 'Well, I'm very pleased that you at least are beginning to see sense. But tell me, what's brought on this change of mind?'

'Like I said it was partly what you said in the hospital and partly because I've been thinking about what that poor girl's parents are suffering. Samantha's got their daughter's heart so in a way they are one and the same now. We owe them all the help we can give.'

For an instant his eyes remained fixed on hers. 'Do you know Karen, I think that's one of the bravest things I've ever heard.' Not really sure whether he actually believed that or had said it simply because he thought she wanted to hear it.

'Kate. My name's Kate. You called me Karen.'

'Did I? Sorry. Slip of the tongue.' But inside he knew it was deeper than that. He was struggling not to visualise this woman before him as his Karen, the only woman he had ever truly loved; the woman taken from him by a car thief, mown down as she fled from a vile, violent man who only wanted to abuse her and kill her and use her remains for profit.

'Do you think your husband will agree? He was fairly emphatic in the hospital.'

'I honestly don't know. All I can do is talk to him.'

'And you'll let me know?'

'Of course.'

'Right then...' Ray stood to leave and as he did so Kate Lowe rose too. For a few seconds they were inches apart, within touching distance. He caught the faint aroma of her body, some kind of scented body lotion perhaps, and suppressed a sudden urge to kiss her on the cheek. That was a gesture for loved ones, for friends, not for someone you had met only briefly but reminded you heart-achingly of someone else.

As he reached the front door, she stretched around him and opened the lock. So close.

'OK Mrs Lowe' — formal this time, to make sure the mistake wasn't repeated — 'I'll wait to hear from you. Call me when you're ready.'

He had barely got the receiver to his ear before he found himself drowning in a tidal wave of invective. 'Just what the fuck do you think you're playing at, you useless lump of shit,' was how it began. 'I've already said no and no means fucking no. What're you trying to do? Going behind my back. Trying to soften up my missus. Well it won't fucking work...'

It took Ray Wilson a few seconds to realise that the voice on the other end of the line belonged to Peter Lowe. He twice tried to stem the torrent but each time the deluge overwhelmed him. Finally he decided to sit back and let it run its course. Eventually the flood of calumny slowed to a trickle.

'Well?' Peter Lowe barked.

'Mr Lowe, I can understand why you may be upset,' began Ray.

'Upset? Upset? Upset doesn't even begin to cover it. I could have you fucking sacked...' And on it went. But after another minute or so the tsunami that was Peter Lowe abated and Ray was able to get a word in.

'Mr Lowe, I don't know what your wife has told you but it was her who rang me, not the other way round,' he said. 'She said she wanted to help; that she would let me speak to Samantha and that she would speak to you about getting you to agree too.'

'Oh she spoke to me about it alright. Caused a flaming great row. I'm not having it.'

'The thing is Mr Lowe that somehow or other, by a process I won't pretend to understand, Samantha knows things that could be critical to the investigation of the murder of another child,' Ray went on. 'Just put yourself in the place of that child's parents. What would you think if another little girl had some information, some knowledge, no matter how tenuous, that might help catch your daughter's killer but that little girl's father wouldn't let the police talk to her? Wouldn't you want the police to do everything they could to persuade him?'

'Yes. My daughter is having problems, terrible psychological problems and I'll do anything to make them go away. But I just can't risk you making them worse.'

Ray played his trump card. 'Mr Lowe, I'm not a psychiatrist and I don't even know if this is true, but have you considered the possibility that if we catch whoever it was that killed Kylie Morris, Samantha's problems might just come to an end? That it might be a closure of some kind or other?'

Peter Lowe, his voice suddenly quietened, said simply, 'Let me think about it. Give me a couple of days.' And he hung up.

Ray waited three days before he made his move. In the pub after work, he button-holed Jan Holroyd.

'I've got a little job for you tomorrow Jan. Right up your street.'

'And what might that be Guv?' she asked.

'I want you to go over to Manchester and see Peter Lowe,' replied Ray. 'I think he might be on the verge of changing his mind about letting us speak to Samantha. And I've got the feeling he might just respond better to the female touch.'

'That's a bit of a sexist thing to say, if you don't mind me saying so Guv,' shot back the DS.

'I know. And it's also a bit of a compliment. I think you're probably the only person on the squad with the ability to pull it off.'

'Guv, you say the sweetest things,' she mocked, draining the remains of her half pint of lager. 'Am I taking anybody with me?'

'No. This one's down to you.'

The following day dragged by; Ray found himself unable to concentrate, glancing continually at the clock until at last it ticked towards five o'clock. Jan Holroyd appeared at his open office door.

'Right Guv, I'm off. Any last minute instructions?'

'No. Just come back with his consent and the gins are on me.'

'Actually I'm more of a vodka girl myself.'

'Alright. Vodka it is. Just do it.'

'Do you want me to ring you when I know, whichever way it goes?' she asked.

Ray glanced at the clock again. 'Yes, you'd better. I can't stand these 100-minute hours for much longer.'

Back home Ray tried to lose himself in the television but all he could find to watch were soaps or so-called 'reality' programmes. He tried the radio but couldn't find anything to suit his mood. Eventually he settled for a large glass of single malt and a paperback written by one of those popular American authors who told an implausible tale moderately well in a manner that didn't demand too much concentration. But no matter how hard he tried, he couldn't stop his eyes straying to the clock. It was gone nine o'clock. Where was she? Surely it couldn't take this long.

Even though he had been anticipating it, when his mobile phone finally did ring, it startled him and he felt the pulse of adrenalin in his blood. 'Yes' he said loudly, pressing the answer button without even bothering to notice who was calling.

'Guv, it's me,' Jan said.

'Yes Jan. How'd it go?' Subtly, Ray was picking up the distinctive Yorkshire dialect.

'OK. I think Thunderbirds are go.'

'What?'

'He says he'll do it.'

'Jan, that's bloody marvellous. I could kiss you.'

'Steady on Guv. And anyway, I'm still in Manchester.'

'Brilliant work Jan. What did you say to him?'

'Oh, it didn't take much,' said Jan self-deprecatingly. 'You know I don't go in for all that psychological bollocks so I just told him that if he didn't co-operate I'd charge him with obstructing the police. Seemed to do the trick.'

'Fuck me Jan,' Ray answered, seeing his new career coming to an abrupt halt. 'Tell me you didn't.'

'Joke Guv, joke. It seems our Mr Lowe made contact with Frank Morris and told him we'd been in touch. They met up at a service area on the M62 and now they're best buddies. He wants to do everything he can to help catch whoever killed Kylie.'

'So what happens now?'

'I said me and you would go back tomorrow evening to talk to Samantha.'

CHAPTER 12

There was an air of unreality in the Lowe's neat home, the tension in the air so tangible that Jan imagined bolts of lightning would flash from her fingertips if she dared touch anything. After the initial greetings and a politely refused invitation to a drink — 'Tea? Coffee? Or something a bit stronger?' — there had been no attempt at conversation. Jan, Ray and the Lowes sat on opposite sides of the living room, words unspoken, almost as if both parties expected what was to follow to be conducted by telepathy.

After a few moments, stretched into infinity by the silence, Peter Lowe simply said: 'I'll go and get her.'

Then suddenly, there she was, looking exactly as she had last time the detectives had seen her. Her blonde hair was swept back, cascading down to her shoulder-blades and she was wearing a pink track suit and white leather trainers.

Before either of the child's parents could say anything, Ray spoke first. 'Hello Samantha. Do you know who I am?'

The little girl fixed him with a stare beyond her years. 'Yes. You're the man who shouted at my Daddy in hospital.'

'I didn't shout at him, I shouted to him. It's different.'

'No it's not.'

'Great,' thought Jan. 'Ten seconds in and he's already got us a hostile witness.'

'The thing is Samantha, we're police officers,' she said, hastily trying to recover the situation. 'And we're working on a case that we think you might be able to help us with. Do you understand what I'm saying?'

'I think so,' replied Samantha.

'That's very good,' Jan said. 'What we're going to do is ask you some questions that we need you to answer as honestly as you can. You understand what honestly means don't you?'

A suddenly timid voice replied: 'Yes. It means I mustn't tell a lie.'

'That's right. It's very important that you tell us the truth. And if we ask you a question that you don't know the answer to, just tell us you don't know. It won't matter but it's very important that you don't tell us something because you think it's what we want to hear. Is that OK?'

'Yes.'

'You've been having some bad dreams haven't you?' began Jan.

'Yes. They frighten me but I can't stop them.'

'And in these dreams, is something bad happening to you?'

Samantha bit her bottom lip and dread filled her eyes. 'Yes. No. It's not me all of the time,' she said. 'It's what I've been telling everybody. It's not just me. There's another little girl.'

It was Ray's turn. He spoke calmly and reassuringly. 'But you're there aren't you Samantha?'

'Yes.'

'And is this other little girl always there too?'

'Most of the time. She wasn't at first, but now I can see her.'

'Can you tell us what this girl looks like?' asked Ray.

'Just normal.'

'Normal? What's normal to you? Tell me,' he said, his voice rising.

Jan anxiously intervened: 'You told the doctors that she had red hair. Is there anything else you can tell us about her?'

'She's older than me.'

'That's very good,' said Jan. 'How much older would you say?'

'I don't know. A bit.'

'Think a bit harder Samantha,' said Ray. 'See if you can think how much older than you she is.'

'I don't know. It's hard.'

'Well, is she one year older than you, or two or three or more?'

'I don't know. More than three, but she's not grown up.'

'Thank you Samantha,' Jan interrupted, sensing that even at this early stage her boss was beginning to lose patience. 'In your dreams, can you see what this other little girl is wearing?'

The look of dread in the child's eyes deepened. 'No. I only see her face. And sometimes it comes close and frightens me.'

Ray, once again calm and reassuring, asked, 'Is that when you can hear her speaking?'

'No. She never says anything when she's close. She's just crying. I think she wants something but I don't know what it is. I'm frightened of her.'

'You told your Mummy that you'd seen a man in your dream,' Ray went on. 'Can you tell us what he looks like?'

The little girl's lip began to curl and Jan feared she was about to burst into tears. Instead she answered: 'Not really. But he's very big. And his hair's really short.'

Inside Ray's head, a red neon light was flashing 'Result'. To his mind, the description matched Robert Craymer. The fact it also matched thousands of other men in West Yorkshire conveniently did not register.

'And you said he was about to hit you. What with?'

This time the tears did flow. Samantha simply yelled 'Mummy' and threw her arms around her mother's neck.

'Samantha, can you see what it is?' pressed Ray. 'Is it round or square or...'

Peter Lowe was on his feet. 'I think that's enough Mr Wilson.'

'But we're just...'

'I said that's enough.'

Ray realised the interview was over. For now. He needed more and he would come back to get it.

As Kate carried her devastated daughter towards the stairs, Ray called out to her, 'Samantha I'm sorry I upset you. I didn't mean to. I hope we can still be friends.'

Peter was already holding the front door open. 'I think you should leave now,' he said.

'I understand,' replied Ray. 'But we'd like to come back and speak to Samantha again.'

'We'll have to see about that. You can see what it does to her. And you don't have to live with the consequences.'

Jan's calming voice said, 'Mr Lowe, we can see how upsetting this is for Samantha and for all of you. But it's been very helpful and it's important that we have the opportunity to speak to your daughter again. We can do it wherever you want. Please think about it. Samantha could be vitally important to our inquiry.'

'I know that,' said Peter. 'I've already promised Frank Morris we'll do everything we can to help the police. But I just can't stand to see her upset.' And with that he closed the door in their faces.

He knew at once that the pub he had chosen was a mistake. Solidly built in local stone with hanging baskets of flowers and a neat little garden off to the side, it stood just outside one of the many pretty villages that dot the moorland between Leeds and Manchester. It was an attractive place and the car park showed it was a popular one too.

But he knew exactly what he would find inside. Couples. Almost all of them married, but not necessarily to each other. Was he pushing things too far? Should he call her and arrange to meet her somewhere else? Or should he simply call the whole thing off? He reached for his mobile phone and as he did so a small, bright red hatchback pulled onto the car park. Kate Lowe was behind the wheel.

Less than 48 hours had passed since Peter Lowe had all but thrown him out of his house and now here he was, out of regular office hours, meeting the man's wife in a moorland pub. At the very least it was unprofessional and could even be construed as misconduct. Yet deep inside Ray knew he had to see Kate Lowe again — and not just for reasons connected to the investigation into Kylie Morris's murder.

He smiled at the woman in the red car who had parked next to him. He smiled at the woman who looked so familiar it hurt. He smiled at the woman he had no right to meet. And she smiled back at him.

'Good evening Chief Inspector," she said as she locked her car.

'Whoa. That's a bit formal,' he replied. 'Please, call me Ray. But look, I'm not sure this is the right place for this. Perhaps we should make it a bit more formal. An office or something.'

'What's the matter? Frightened of getting caught with a married woman,' she said, in a manner that Ray momentarily thought over-familiar.

'No. It's just that I'm not sure the location is appropriate.'

'Oh, come on. We're here now,' she said. 'And it does look like a very nice pub.'

Against his better judgement he led the way across the stone-flagged entrance hall into a lounge bar that could have been in any country pub anywhere in England. The floor was covered by a red and gold carpet that was once thickly piled but was now worn thin and threadbare in places. There were stout wooden beams, some original, some obviously fairly recent additions, 'distressed' to make them look old, but all of them covered in horse brasses, sepia-toned photographs and framed documents purporting to display the 'Rules of the Inn' and 'Bill of Fayre.'

The clientele was exactly as he had expected. The tables in the centre of the room were largely unoccupied while around the perimeter couples sat staring into each other's eyes, some of them guiltily, some with undisguised lust. Some of them held hands surreptitiously.

It had been a long time since he had been on his own in a pub with a woman. At the bar he quickly chose one of the several cask beers on offer and ordered a pint and, without asking, a gin and tonic with ice and lemon.

'Ray, sorry but I don't like gin. And anyway, I'm driving.' The Manchester accent suddenly brought him back from wherever he was. 'I'll have an orange juice please.'

'Course. Sorry. I should've asked,' was the best he could manage.

They took their drinks to a table for four in the middle of the room and sat on opposite sides, as if making a deliberate statement to their fellow drinkers. For the next hour they made small-talk, exchanging the who, what, why and whens that make up the minutiae of life but by the end of it Ray knew little more about Kate Lowe than he did at the beginning. Not because she hadn't been forthcoming, but because he hadn't been listening. His mind had been in another pub, in another county with another woman.

Eventually, on his third pint, he got round to the official reason for meeting her. He needed her to persuade her husband once more.

'I'm really sorry about the other day,' he started. 'It was my fault. I went too far with Samantha...'

'I don't think Pete helped much,' she interrupted.

'No, but he was right,' Ray said. 'I appreciate she's in a pretty fragile state but she's so important to this inquiry. I just got carried away. I'm sure you understand. It's very frustrating when you come up against a brick wall in an investigation. And right now Samantha's my only way of getting over that wall.'

'I know. And we really want to help. We even promised Frank — that's Kylie's Dad — that we'd do everything we could but you have to understand how we feel.' Kate began to fidget with something she was holding. It took a few seconds for Ray to realise it was a small lace handkerchief.

'Samantha's our only child. She was born seriously ill and we very nearly lost her. We're only too aware that she's only alive because of Kylie. But she's so precious we can't do anything that puts her at risk.'

Ray picked up his pint. 'But we only want to talk to her; to find out what's in her head. There's a theory which states that when she received Kylie's heart she also took on part of her memory. It sounds incredible but the doctors seem to believe it and I have to say I think there might be something in it.'

'But what if it causes her permanent damage?' Kate dabbed her eyes with the handkerchief.

'I know that's a risk,' Ray replied. 'But there must be a way we can find out if she knows anything of value without doing her any lasting harm. That's all I want. Another chance. Will you talk to Peter?'

He could see that her mind was in turmoil, torn between keeping her daughter safe and allowing her to be used to catch a violent, predatory killer. Her eyes played around his face as her brain rapidly reached for a solution.

'I'll talk to him, yes,' she said. 'But I can't guarantee which way he'll go. I think it will depend a lot on what the doctors say but, then again, he's promised Frank to do whatever he can.'

Ray knew that was the best response he could hope for. He glanced at his watch. Almost nine o'clock. Time for her to be getting back home.

'Thank you Karen, I...'

'That's the second time you've done that.'

'Done what?'

'Called me Karen. You did it the first time you came to the house. My name's Kate.'

'Sorry, of course it is. Slip of the tongue.'

'Who is she then, this Karen?'

'Just someone I used to know. She's...It's not important.' The lie lanced his heart but he didn't feel able to tell Kate the truth. At least not yet. 'Come on. It's time both of us were going.'

CHAPTER 13

The feeling began to flood over him as he sat, alone, watching his favourite film on his precious 50-inch plasma screen. It was one of those cheaply made American movies that consisted of little more than sustained gratuitous violence, no discernible plot and no characterisation, that had gone straight to DVD to be watched only by men like him.

But as he watched, images floated around his mind; images from his own memory; images that should have tormented him but actually gave him a sort of satisfaction. Even now he was amazed at how easy it had been. He hadn't set out to do it. The original idea had been simply to teach a bitch of a woman a lesson she wouldn't forget. Things had got out of hand though because once he'd started, he found himself enjoying it, so he carried on. And on. And on.

Finally the kid stopped crying and screaming; stopped pleading; stopped begging. She stopped everything that had made it fun so he cut her down, firmly believing she was dead. A whack round the back of the head with the heavy length of timber he'd used to batter her body should have made sure of it. But just in case she came round while he was driving her to where he was going to dump her body, he gagged her with a length of the duct-tape he'd brought from home and used a couple of cable ties to bind her wrists and ankles.

When TV news reported that she was still alive when a group of mountain bikers found her, he experienced a moment of panic and then he remembered what he'd learned from watching all those drama series that purported to give away the tricks of forensic science. He believed there would be no fingerprints because he had worn latex gloves every time he touched her. He believed there would be no DNA because he wore a condom when he raped her. If the cops did knock on his door he would just bluff it out because he knew they would have nothing they could pin on him.

But all that had been weeks ago. And now this feeling was coursing through him; a feeling he could not control and, even if he could, it was a feeling he did not want to control. His very skin tingled at the excitement the feeling produced. He imagined lightning bolts jagging across his brain. The feeling had become an urge; an urge he was compelled to obey.

He had to kill again.

This time though, it would be planned. He'd drive out of the city and look for a young girl in one of the more remote towns and villages. He couldn't take the risk of lying in wait for someone, in case some nosy parker saw him so he'd take the first one that fitted the bill, which, even he admitted to himself, was not too long. Between 10 and 13 was all it took. Hair colour didn't matter. A school uniform would be nice but not vital.

Then he'd do exactly what he did with the first one. He'd take her to the same place and give her exactly the same treatment, except this time, hanging her up by her arms and battering her, first with his fists and then with a piece of wood, would not be done in anger as an act of revenge. It would be done as a considered act to cause pain and terror and bring him to the point of arousal at which he could rape her.

The first kid would probably be alive today if she hadn't spat in his face. His plan had been to keep her for a week or so, just to show that bitch of a mother of hers who was boss; to frighten the shit out of her. But when he removed her gag so he could spoon feed her tomato soup, she spat at him. Spitting at someone. What a disgusting thing to do. He couldn't think of anything worse. The very thought of it made him want to vomit. He had felt the spittle run down his cheek and as an impulsive reaction he smashed his fist into her tear-streaked face.

And so it began.

Tomorrow was Saturday. Quieter roads. No mums on the school run. A more relaxed day all round.

A good day to take his next victim.

Most of his fellow citizens were still sleeping, the pavements and side streets deserted as he set off on his quest. There was no real reason to be out this early, other than he was finding it difficult to contain his excitement. And an early start would give him time to choose his spot. He knew that the police were aware of the red Ford Transit Connect but a hundred quid payment to a mate who knew a bit about spray painting had resulted in a passing, but not perfect, colour change to the outside of the van. He had taken off the identifying badges, including the ones that just said 'Ford,' in the belief that the vast majority of the public would not recognise one brand of small boxy van from another.

His confidence in his own ability to strike again unnoticed was high.

Of the perils posed to his freedom by the thousands of cat hairs that carpeted the hovel he called home, he remained blissfully unaware.

His journey took him around Bradford's ring road, then north through the small towns of Bingley and Keighley, both of which he briefly considered and rejected as potential locations. Almost 20 miles and more than 30 minutes after he'd left home, he drove into Skipton, the town that calls itself 'The Gateway to the Yorkshire Dales.' It had been a long time since he was last here and he'd forgotten how pretty it was. He drove through streets that were beginning to bustle and decided this was a good place; a good place to satisfy the urge that was still strong inside him.

Turning a corner he was confronted by a brown sign with white lettering and a direction arrow; a tourist information sign. It said: 'Craven Swimming Pool.'

He followed the sign and found himself on a reasonably sized car park, surrounded by parklands and screened from the main road by trees. At the far end was the modern swimming pool.

Perfect.

He settled down to wait, just another vehicle among the 20 or so already parked. The first kids that emerged were a couple of young boys. No good. It had to be a girl. Other boys followed, some of them slouching along, their faces hidden in hoodies, others laughing and joking with each other. He had begun to think that maybe he had stumbled on a boys-only swimming session and that he should probably move on when he saw her.

He could see she was about 12 years-old, trying her best to be fashionable in black leggings, denim shorts and a loosely fitting sweater. Her long black hair, still wet from the pool, glistened over her shoulders. She carried a bright yellow sports bag. And she was walking towards him.

As she got closer he got out. 'Hiya. You don't know me but I live round the corner from you,' he said. 'Your mum asked me if I'd mind picking you up.'

It didn't occur to her to ask his name or how he knew her mum. It didn't occur to her to ask how her mum knew what time she would be out of the pool. It didn't occur to her that this was anything more than a friendly neighbour, even though she didn't know him from Adam.

All she said was: 'Oh, thanks' and climbed in.

And from the moment the van door closed, her fate was sealed.

CHAPTER 14

Jim Bibby had spent his life farming the uncompromising uplands of the Yorkshire Dales. Born and raised on the farm he now owned after inheriting it from his father, he was physically tough and mentally in tune with everything that went on around him. He prided himself on knowing every square foot of the 120 acres over which his sheep and cattle grazed.

This morning, just like every other morning, he was out of bed before 5am and 20 minutes later — after a splash of cold water and slurp of hot tea — he was in the shippon milking his small herd of cows. The yield was not much but it was collected everyday by two blokes who had set up a creamery to make cheese. The money it brought in wasn't much either but at least it was something. He knew other farmers in the Dales who had to throw their milk away because they couldn't sell it.

Then it was time to check on his sheep; to make sure the ewes were in the best condition for breeding; to check that his flock was properly fed and watered and that there were no holes in the dry limestone walls that would allow them to escape. His tractor had seen better days but it still served its purpose and could still muster the power to drag along heavily-laden trailers when it needed to. Anyway, even a decent second hand one was beyond him and the banks wouldn't help with a loan. But he had faith that if he stuck to the ritual, it would start, just like it did every day.

Turn the ignition key and watch for the glow-plug indicator to go out, showing it's at the right temperature to fire the diesel engine. Meanwhile, pump the throttle three times and dip the clutch twice. Close your eyes and press the 'start' button. The engine bursts into life, accompanied by a thick billowing cloud of blue-black smoke from the exhaust and Bob's your uncle.

Jim drove across the farmyard and along the short track that led to the road where he turned right and headed off over a shoulder of the moor with its exposed limestone pavements, which reflected the early morning sunlight. This was what he loved. The peace; the quiet; the open countryside as far as he could see. And his land. His land that belonged to his father before him and his father before that. To Jim's reckoning, this was as close to Heaven on earth as it was possible to get.

He knew at once that whatever it was he was looking at didn't belong there. On foot he probably would not have seen it, but from the elevated position of his tractor cab he could see that something had been dumped in one of his fields.

It was just a few feet from the dry-stone wall, close to the tubular steel gate that prevented his livestock wandering on to the narrow, little-used moorland road. And it hadn't been there yesterday, of that he was certain.

His first thought as he stopped the tractor was *'Bloody townies dumping their rubbish again.'*

He lifted the blue nylon cord that provided a fastening for the gate and walked towards the bundle, which at first glance he took to be a pile of clothes. But as he got closer, he realised that the pile of clothes also had hair; long, dark hair, matted with mud and blood.

Instinctively, he turned the bundle over — and leapt back in revulsion at what he saw.

A human body, a young human body, he had no doubt. But the features had been so disfigured he couldn't tell whether it was a boy or a girl, the injuries so horrific even his untrained eye could tell that the youngster had suffered a terrible beating.

He fled back to his tractor where trembling hands found his mobile phone easily enough but took two attempts to dial 999.

Ray was having another frustrating day of nothingness. He had heard nothing from Kate and Peter Lowe. He had heard nothing from Richard Fairfax or Stephen Parke. He had heard nothing from any of the team he had working on the murder of Kylie Morris. And nothing was exactly what he felt like doing for the rest of the day. Then he saw Jan Holroyd scurrying towards his office at a speed that implied she was being chased.

She gave a cursory knock on the glass door and barged in. 'Guv, looks like we've got another.'

'What? Another what?'

'Another dead girl Guv,' said Jan. 'Up in the Dales. Farmer found her first thing this morning dumped in a field. Similar injuries to Kylie too by the sound of it.'

'Hang on Jan,' Ray said, trying to slow down his sergeant. 'Who's telling us this?'

'I've just had a call from North Yorkshire,' she replied. 'A farmer near Grassington found the body and she's been informally identified as Zoe Clayton, aged 13, reported missing from home in Skipton three days ago.

'They rang us because of the similarities with our case. She'd been severely beaten with something heavy. And she'd been raped. There were quite a few tyre tracks at the scene but — and this is the good bit Guv — preliminary investigation shows that one of them could be a match for the tracks we found on The Chevin.'

For a moment Ray didn't move. He stared at Jan Holroyd with a look that could have been incomprehension or simply a wish not to believe what he had just heard. Another child had been murdered — bearing the hallmarks of Kylie Morris's killer.

Finally he said, 'Right. I need to speak to whoever's in charge up there and quickly. Get me the details.'

Five minutes later, he was talking to Detective Chief Inspector Paul Connors.

'I appreciate you letting us know about this,' Ray began, 'but just to make sure it isn't a coincidence, there are a few details you need to know that we've not made public. But first of all, when's the post-mortem being done?

Connors replied, 'It should be starting anytime now. Is there something we should be looking for?

'Yes, although it might sound a bit bonkers,' Ray said. 'Ask your pathologist to look for cat hairs.'

'Cat hairs? You serious?'

'Deadly. Get a call through to the pathologist then call me back and I'll tell you what else you need to know.'

Ray just had time to make a cup of tea before Connors called back. 'Right, I've spoken to the doc and asked him to keep an eye open for cat hairs,' he said, 'so what else should I know?'

'OK, let me start at the beginning,' said Ray, clicking open a computer file and putting his feet up on the desk.

For the next 20 minutes he told Connors how Kylie Morris had found bound, gagged, beaten, raped and dumped barely alive. He explained how the pathologist, Dr Skuse, had concluded that despite the severity of her injuries, which indicated she had been hanged by the arms, the cause of death was blunt force trauma caused by a blow from a piece of unplanned timber about 200 millimetres square. He told how there was no semen present on Kylie's body, indicating that the person who raped her had used a condom. He told how a tyre track had been found close by and how a witness had later come forward to say he had seen Kylie getting into a red Ford Transit Connect and how a search for the vehicle had so far proved fruitless. He told how a forensic examination of the duct tape used to gag her had revealed cat hairs and how scientists had said DNA checks could be used to identify the animals they had come from, even though that line of inquiry had also been fruitless. He told his counterpart that Robert Craymer remained a person of interest but that no evidence had been found against him.

He did not tell Connors of the existence of Samantha Lowe and he did not tell him of the fantastical theory of cellular memory advanced by the two doctors treating her for the terrible nightmares she was suffering.

Ray concluded the conversation by saying: 'I'd be obliged if you could let me have a copy of the pathologist's report and, of course, if you do find any cat hairs, let me know at once so we can cross check DNA.'

'I have to admit that the cat hair connection is a new one on me,' Connors replied. 'But we'll see what we can find and let you know.'

Twenty four hours later, Connors rang Ray to tell him the results of Zoe Clayton's post mortem — and it was depressingly familiar. The pathologist had established that, despite the severe beating she had received, the cause of death had been at least two blows to the back of her head with a piece of unplanned timber, about 200 millimetres square. Her inner thighs showed signs of bruising consistent with her having been raped, although there was no semen present. There were abrasions on her wrists, and the muscles of her upper arms and shoulders were torn, injuries that the pathologist had said could have been caused by the little girl being hanged by her arms.

'What about cat hairs? Did you find any cat hairs?' Ray demanded.

'I'm coming to that,' Connors replied calmly. 'There's something else that may interest you too. The wounds to the back of Zoe's head contained fibres from the unplanned timber, as you would expect. But they also contained human hair that's not from Zoe. It's red and hers was black. Plus, there was what appears to be a single hair that's not human. The doc's doing some tests right now but he's said he's fairly certain it's cat hair.'

There was a few seconds silence while Ray absorbed what he'd been told, then, with no explanation: 'The bastard.' He quickly followed up by asking: 'Can you get your forensic guys to get a DNA sample from the cat hair and let the mob that's taken over from the Forensic Science Service in Wetherby have it so they can do a cross-check?'

'That's easy enough,' replied Connors. 'We're using the same lab.'

Ray's next call was to Stephen Parke. He had to get the medics to agree to him questioning Samantha Lowe. The parents, he knew, would be reluctant, but if the doctors said the interview could take place, he was convinced they would let it go ahead, if only for no other reason than they had promised Frank Morris they would do everything they could to help catch Kylie's killer.

He had no idea how Stephen Parke would react, but he was certain he would not be greeted like a long-lost brother and he was right.

'I was hoping never to hear from you again,' was Parke's opening shot. 'I know you went sneaking behind my back and persuaded Mrs Lowe that you should talk to Samantha. And I know the state you left her in. You're very lucky I haven't reported you to a higher authority...'

Ray interrupted the flow of invective. 'Mr Parke, whatever has gone between us before is now largely immaterial. Whoever killed Kylie Morris has done it again. He's killed another little girl in exactly the same manner. So it's now imperative that I'm permitted to speak to Samantha and ask her more questions. If you say no I am of a mind to go to court and get an order to force you.' Then he shut up.

For several seconds Parke made no response. When he did speak Ray knew he was going to get his way. The aggressive attitude was gone; the harsh edge to the voice softened; the tone almost suppliant. 'Mr Wilson, I'm dreadfully sorry to hear that. I had no idea. Are you sure?'

'As sure as we can be at this stage. Tyre tracks found at the scene match those found at the location where Kylie was found. And there's other forensic evidence that I'm not at liberty to divulge.'

'Of course, of course. I understand. How can I help you?'

'I would have thought that was fairly obvious,' Ray said, recognising that at last he had the upper hand.

'This person has killed twice, both times committing despicable acts on his young victims. We need to catch him before he does it again because, believe me, now he's got the taste sooner or later he will do it again.

'And the person holding to the key to finding him is Samantha. I need to know everything that's in her head.

'I understand your concerns and I don't want to do anything that might have any impact on her future well-being. But I also can't leave this person on the streets. That's why I need your help in dealing with Mr and Mrs Lowe. And I need your advice. Is there anything, any technique, any procedure that you've not yet thought of that might help unlock what's in Samantha's sub-conscious?'

Parke replied, 'I need to do some research; get some help from other people. I'll have to ring you back.'

'That's OK but bear in mind I need to do this interview as quickly as is humanly possible so we can get this bastard.'

He put the phone down with the feeling that for the first time since they met, Stephen Parke was going to play ball.

Then he went out to brief his team about the second murder. To tell them of the matching tyre tracks; the similarities between the circumstances in which the bodies were found and in the injuries the two little girls had suffered.

And that the killer had used the same piece of wood to end both of their lives.

The following night, the discovery of Zoe's battered body was the lead item on the local TV news bulletins. The broadcasts told how she had vanished after leaving the swimming pool in Skipton and how farmer Jim Bibby made his grim discovery three days later. The BBC had managed a brief interview with Zoe's devastated parents, who had described her as "our little angel" and said a light had gone out in their lives. Neighbours and distant relatives queued up to tell the cameras of a bright, bubbly young girl who lived for sport. A girl who was warm and friendly to everyone she met. A girl who would give a helping hand to anyone and who was loved by everybody who knew her.

He stared at his giant television screen, unmoved by the story that was unfolding. A can of strong lager in his hand, two cats curled up in his lap, he listened intently for any hint that the police might have a lead, anything, no matter how tenuous, that might bring them to his door. But as the reporter who had been speaking live from outside Zoe's home handed back to the studio he realised there was nothing. He'd got away with it again. Time for more beer.

Ray, too, watched the news in the comfort of his moorland cottage. But what was being said didn't sink in. It merely provided a background noise for his thoughts which were elsewhere.

He couldn't stop thinking about a woman he couldn't have; a woman he shouldn't have; a woman whose young daughter was fundamental to the most important inquiry of his career, the first murder case he had ever run; a woman he knew he would see again soon.

Work was taking over his life, he realised. He needed something else to occupy the hours he spent alone. He needed to go sailing again. Sailing had been a passion ever since he was a boy in The Fens when his father bought a cruiser for the family to use on the Norfolk Broads, but he hadn't been near a boat since that day in Yarmouth Yacht Station; the day the only woman he had ever loved was taken from him by a social misfit in a stolen car.

Now it was time for him to get his feet wet again. It's what Karen would have wanted.

Ray reached for his laptop and, using both index fingers, he typed "Yacht clubs in Yorkshire" into his search engine. In less time than it takes to blink, the page filled up with responses but as he went through them he quickly realised that most of them were dinghy sailing clubs. His dinghy sailing days were well behind him. Competitive dinghy sailing was a young man's sport and in Ray's mind there was only one reason to step onto a sailing boat and that was to go racing.

He loved the freedom that came with being at sea. He loved pitching himself against whatever nature threw his way, making the most of the weather, good or bad. And he loved the camaraderie and the banter that came with being a member of a crew of seven, eight or more. He needed to go racing on a keelboat.

The list that had been revealed to him featured only four yacht clubs on the Yorkshire coast. For the next hour or so he carefully studied each of their websites, mentally marking positives and negatives for each one before settling on Whitby Yacht Club as his first choice.

Whitby. The only things he knew about the place was that it was the town in which Count Dracula landed in Bram Stoker's famous Victorian horror story and that it had a ruined abbey on a cliff-top. Another Internet search revealed it was also the home of Captain James Cook, the 18th century explorer credited with discovering Australia and that it boasted a renowned fish-and-chip shop.

When Saturday finally arrived, he spent at least an hour scrabbling around his cottage looking for his sailing gear, which he found stowed in odd cupboards and drawers all over the house. Making a mental note to look after his kit better, he threw his battered bag into the boot alongside a small overnight bag before heading east, around the outskirts of Leeds, then York and through the North Yorkshire National Park into Whitby.

The yacht club was on Pier Road, overlooking the historic harbour, with the imposing ruins of St Mary's Church on the headland above. It wasn't the flashiest yacht club he had ever seen but he knew at once that he would be comfortable there and that he would be accepted, not because of what car he drove or how much he earned, but because of his love of sailing and what he could do on a boat.

Two hours later he'd been given the 'grand tour' — which took all of 10 minutes — met four or five of the members, had a beer or two and got himself onto a 34-foot boat for the following day's race. He could feel calm and contentment coursing through his veins as he checked in to a bed-and-breakfast hotel run by a relative of one of the bar staff.

By the time the race started on Sunday, Ray's mind was concentrated on doing what he loved doing best — helping to make a boat go quickly. Kylie Morris, Zoe Clayton, Stephen Parke and Richard Fairfax were not on his radar. Neither was Kate Lowe. And for the first time in months, neither was his beloved Karen.

CHAPTER 15

It was a new Ray who bounded into his office on Monday morning. He was in a notably good mood, sporting a smile and with a lightness of step that indicated a man who had spent the weekend enjoying himself.

'Must have had his leg over,' observed one of the younger detectives to no one in particular.

'That's enough Barnes,' chided Jan Holroyd. 'That's the boss you're talking about.'

'I was just...'

'Yeah, well don't.'

'Yeah, Barnsey,' chipped in another detective. 'Careful we don't start talking about your sex life. Mind you, it wouldn't take long.'

'Cheeky bugger. I'll have you know I've done it three times this weekend,' he countered.

'Yeah, but the question is, was anyone else involved?' quipped Jan, theatrically raising an eyebrow.

Barnes' face matched the colour of his red socks.

In his office Ray was confronted with a stack of paper work: reports, letters, expenses claims, overtime chits, none of which could be ignored. And when he switched on his computer, it showed him he had 31 e-mails to wade through as well.

'It's a bloody miracle any crimes get solved at all with all this crap to deal with,' he thought, heading off towards the small kitchen to make a cup of strong tea.

As he waited for the kettle to boil he realised that the feeling of euphoria that had glided him into work was rapidly receding and he was briefly gripped by a longing for a simpler life, a life in which there was no stack of paper work, no e-mails, no aggravation.

Back behind his desk, he had barely had time for a sip of the dark brown liquid in his mug before the urgent shrill of the telephone demanded his attention.

'Wilson,' he barked into the handset, the name exploding much more aggressively than was his intention.

'Mr Wilson, good morning. It's Richard Fairfax.' The quiet, carefully modulated voice took Ray by surprise. Richard Fairfax was the last person he expected to hear from on a Monday morning.

There was a fraction of a second of silence, but before Ray had the chance to say anything Fairfax continued. 'Stephen has told me of the developments in your case. They're deeply disturbing and I want you to know that I, personally, will do whatever I can to help. I know we've had our differences in the past but in the final analysis I believe we're both after the same goal. You want to catch a murderer and I want to help a little girl suffering extreme mental torment. To my mind the two are inextricably linked.'

'Well, thank you Dr Fairfax. I'm delighted that you have come round to seeing things my way at last.'

'Oh, I've always seen things your way, as you put it,' said Fairfax. 'It's just your methods of getting there that I questioned.'

'I don't think...' But before Ray could start an argument, Fairfax cut him off.

'Stephen told me you'd asked him whether there were any new techniques or procedures that might help your investigation. Well, there is one I know of. It's called Eye Movement Desensitisation and Reprocessing, or EMDR for short.

'It's not exactly new — it was first tried in America on Vietnam veterans suffering Post Traumatic Stress Disorder — but it hasn't been used much in this country. I'm familiar with the theory but I must confess I've never used it myself. If we decide to go ahead and try the technique on Samantha I'll need to do a lot more research.'

Ray couldn't resist. 'If you don't mind me saying so doc, it sounds like another theory straight from the Cellular Memory farm.'

'Don't be deceived Mr Wilson. This technique has had proven success in America and in other parts of Europe and on the few occasions it's been used in this country. But it's a technique that requires specialist knowledge to administer so if you want to go ahead, I'll need to find someone with the qualifications to do it.'

'OK,' said Ray. 'But how does it work?'

'On the face of it, it's remarkably simple,' Fairfax began. 'The basis of the therapy is to stimulate both halves of the brain simultaneously by using light or sound that tracks left to right and back again. It's thought that this emulates the psychological state during Rapid Eye Movement — REM — sleep. Studies have shown that when we're in REM sleep we make new associations between things very rapidly — a kind of high-speed processing, if you will.

'In expert hands, it means even the most traumatic of episodes can be broken down into small chunks, which in turn helps the process of dealing with that trauma as painless as possible.'

'Do you think it will really work with Samantha?'

'I've no idea. But I do think it's the best chance we've got of unlocking whatever it is that's causing her problems. I know EMDR has been used on children suffering from nightmares. Whether it will work on a fragile little girl who is suffering someone else's nightmare, I just don't know, but I do know we owe it to her to try.'

'All you have to do now is persuade Mr and Mrs Lowe to let you go ahead.'

'No need,' said Fairfax. 'They've already agreed to let me try it. And what's more, they've agreed to let you witness the whole thing yourself.'

Ray felt his heart leap. He was going to see her again, without having to engineer a reason. He was going to talk to her, stand close to her, smell her scent, breath the same air that she breathed. Maybe even have physical contact. The heavy grey cloud of depression that was beginning to settle on him before the conversation began blew away.

'That's great news doc. So where do we go from here.'

'Well, it's now my job to identify a therapist with the right experience,' said Fairfax. 'Once I've done that we can make the necessary arrangements to try the therapy on Samantha. I'll be back in touch when I have more news.'

As the telephone dropped back on its cradle, the rapture that had enveloped him earlier returned. Stupid to let little things like admin get him down. Think positive, that's what he needed to do. There was now a bright star on his horizon to steer for. Time for more tea, he thought.

Such was the elation that gripped him as he stepped out into the squad room clutching his empty mug that instead of shouting for someone to make a new one, he called out: 'Anyone want a brew?'

For a fraction of second, the surprise silenced the handful of detectives at their desks. Then, one by one, they began to respond. 'Yeah, cheers Boss.' 'Two sugars Boss.' 'Can I have a coffee please Boss?'

Ten minutes later, he was back in the squad room carrying a tin tray on which were balanced half a dozen mugs, including his own. He set the tray down on an empty desk and announced, 'Brew's up.'

He picked up his own cup and made to walk back into his office. Then he stopped, as if a thought had suddenly struck him.

'By the way Barnsey,' he said, half turning towards the room, 'you were wrong. I didn't get my leg over this weekend but I'm working on it. Just thought you might like to know.'

For the second time in less than an hour, Barnes's face was indistinguishable from his socks.

A week later Ray found himself in an attractive Georgian street in the centre of Manchester, one of the few that had survived the frenzy of demolition and development that had turned most of the surrounding area into a hotchpotch of Identikit glass and steel buildings — square, oblong, tall, curved — in the name of modernisation. Ray was a stranger to the city but he couldn't help thinking that if the architects and planners had done this everywhere, they'd have torn the heart out of the place.

The highly polished brass plaques screwed to each door showed him that what was once a street of elegant houses was now home almost exclusively to lawyers and doctors. He stopped outside the door on which one of the plaques read 'Miriam Tabor FBPsS' and rang the bell. It was answered, after about a minute, by a woman who at first glance could have been anywhere between 30 and 45. She was dressed in an obviously-expensive black pin-striped suit, the skirt of which ended chastely below her knees, a crisp white blouse and a startlingly pink bow tie. He was struck by how tall she appeared, an impression accentuated by the fact she stood a door-step's height above him.

Before she could speak, Ray held up his warrant card. 'Detective Chief Inspector Ray Wilson to see Dr Tabor,' he said.

He saw that her eyes registered disapproval while her mouth — lips highlighted by vivid pink lipstick that matched her bow tie — smiled and said: 'Do come in Mr Wilson. The others are in the waiting room. Can I get you tea or coffee?'

'Er... coffee, no sugar, thank you,' he replied, taken aback by the warmth in her voice that was betrayed by the look in her eye.

As she turned away to lead him to the waiting room, he spotted she was balanced on a pair of bright red, murderously high heels that added considerably to her height and gave her a grace akin to that of a sky-scraper — elegant, but not necessarily attractive.

The first person he saw when he entered the small waiting room was Samantha, wearing the same pink designer track suit and white leather trainers she was the very first time he saw her. The thought crossed his mind — and was instantly dismissed as patently untrue — that maybe it was the only outfit she had. He realised the suit was probably a kind of comfort blanket that the little girl insisted on wearing whenever she had to see a doctor.

Her father, sitting on her right, acknowledged Ray with nothing more than a curt smile and a nod of his head. And then, there she was. Hands held primly on her lap, a touch too much blusher on her cheeks. His first impression was of a delicate China doll. She looked anxious, concerned, and care-worn. But she still looked like Karen and he could feel the colour rising in his face. She managed a smile and a muffled 'Hello' but it was a voice from behind him that was most effusive.

'Mr Wilson, good morning. Good to see you again.' Ray had not expected Richard Fairfax's greeting to be so welcoming. 'Stephen sends his apologies but he thought two of us would be a bit of an over-kill.'

'Good morning doctor and good morning Mr and Mrs Lowe. And Samantha,' Ray said. 'It's kind of you all to let me be here. I...'

Before he could get any further, Sky-Scraper Woman entered and put down a small silver salver on a polished mahogany coffee table in the middle of the room. 'Your coffee Mr Wilson,' was all she said.

On the salver was a bone China cup and saucer, a silver coffee pot, a small silver jug of cream, two matching silver bowls, one containing brown sugar cubes, the other white, a pair of silver tongs and an antique silver Bishop's spoon. No wonder private medicine's so expensive, thought Ray.

Richard Fairfax spoke to everyone. 'Dr Tabor is one of the leading psychologists in the country,' he said. 'She is very experienced in the field of child psychology but specialises in the treatment of trauma cases and uses EMDR therapy frequently. And she's also giving her services free of charge. She's intrigued by Samantha's case, although I have to say she's sceptical about the theory of cellular memory. It will be interesting to see what, if anything, she can achieve.'

Suddenly, Sky-Scraper Woman was back among them. 'Dr Tabor is ready for you now,' she said. 'Please follow me.'

She led the way up two flights of a wide, ornate staircase at the top of which she tapped on a heavy oak door, stepped through and held it open.

Miriam Tabor was sitting behind an imposingly large desk with her back to two full length windows that flooded the room with natural light. To her left, a glass-fronted bookcase filled the length of the wall from floor to ceiling. The right hand side of the room was screened from view by heavy, dark blue velvet curtains. In front of her desk were two small leather armchairs and three hard-backed chairs, obviously brought in for the appointment.

As Richard Fairfax entered first, Dr Tabor rose formally and with a sweep of her left arm said, 'Good morning everybody. Please take a seat. Mr and Mrs Lowe, if you will,' indicating that she wanted them to take the armchairs. Samantha chose to sit on her father's knee, leaving Ray and Fairfax to occupy the hard-back chairs.

The psychologist was in her late 50s with a round, open face that could have indicated Slavic roots. 'Have you all been offered tea, coffee or whatever?' she asked. Despite her obvious desire to put everyone at their ease, a pair of large, heavily framed, square glasses, with blue-tinted lenses gave her a somewhat sinister aspect. Ray noticed that Samantha had drawn herself closer to her father and put an arm across his chest.

'Right. I don't believe in wasting time, so let's get started shall we?' It wasn't so much a question as a statement of intent by Miriam Tabor. 'Richard has filled me in on the background to Samantha's case; her medical history; how these nightmares began after her heart transplant and the police's subsequent interest, although, strictly speaking, this was not necessary for me to be able to conduct the therapy.

'I have to say that I find Richard's theory of cellular memory a little too close to science fiction for my liking but I accept that Samantha's problems only began after her surgery and that her operation may be somehow linked to the trauma she is now suffering. What I do have difficulty with is that Samantha's problems are connected in any way to the murder of a young girl who she had never met and of whom she knew nothing.

'However, I understand that Mr and Mrs Lowe are helping the police and that is why Mr..Mr?'

'Wilson doctor. Detective Chief Inspector Wilson,' said Ray. 'And it's two murders now.'

'Yes, whatever,' Miriam Tabor said. 'That is why Chief Inspector Wilson is here to witness proceedings and to see if anything emerges that may be useful to his enquiries.

'But before we start, I'd just like to explain something about Eye Movement Desensitisation and Reprocessing, or EMDR for short. I don't know how much any of you know of the technique but it is not a magical key that unlocks all the hidden doors in the brain. Nor is it a miracle cure for all psychological problems.

'But it is an effective, proven therapy that has helped more than a million people world-wide who have suffered trauma of one kind or another, including sexual abuse, domestic violence, combat and crime. It has also proved effective in treating those suffering from a variety of other psychological complications including depression, addiction, phobias and self-esteem issues.

'I believe it will be a useful tool in helping to alleviate Samantha's problems. Whether it will help bring a murderer to justice is another matter entirely. Shall we get on with it?'

'It might be useful if you could spend a few minutes explaining, as simply as possible, how EMDR works,' said Fairfax.

The psychologist let out an audible sigh. 'Very well, if that's what you want. Put very simply, the brain is divided into two halves, known as hemispheres. When we are suffering from an issue the right-hand hemisphere, which controls creativity and emotions, is more active than the left-hand, logical hemisphere. EMDR uses light or sound to create bilateral stimulation, which generates activity equally in both halves of the brain. The belief is that this forces more communication through the corpus callosum — if you will, the bridge between the hemispheres — and allows us to access more areas of both sides of the brain simultaneously. The overall effect is that issues and situations can be viewed more objectively and logically, where previously emotions dominated.

'The important thing to remember is that this therapy is patient-led. In other words, Samantha will have full control of the process. I will guide her and occasionally I will stop her to ask questions to help guide her through the process. It will only be complete, and capable of being judged successful, when whatever memory is troubling Samantha has faded into the past and she can look back on it with a positively enhanced sense of well-being. And it's only fair to warn you, it can take several sessions to reach that state.

'Right. Now can we carry on?'

She got up from the desk and opened the heavy curtains that screened the right wall, revealing two hard-backed chairs set on either side of a cross shaped object, made in metal, the cross bar of which was about a metre long and housed a continuous line of small LED lights. The wall behind the lights was painted matt white with not even a blemish to distract attention.

'OK Samantha, will you come over here please sweetheart?' Everyone in the room noticed the change in the tone of Miriam Tabor's voice. Where previously she had been forthright, almost harsh, she was now speaking softly, gently, persuasively. Ray wondered cynically whether she was a one-woman good-cop/bad-cop. 'The rest of you stay where you are and please be quiet.'

When Samantha had settled in the upright chair, the psychologist switched on the machine that faced her. The LED on the extreme left lit up green.

She spoke softly to the little girl: 'Now Samantha, when I switch this machine on properly, the little green light you can see over here will travel right the way along this bar and back again and it will keep doing that until I stop it. What I need you to do is keep your eyes on the light. Don't look anywhere else. Keep looking at the light. That's very important. Do you think you can do that for me?'

Samantha bit her bottom lip and nodded.

'Good. I will ask you some questions while the light is moving and I want you to answer them and tell me your thoughts but don't look at me while you're doing it. Remember, just keep looking at the light. Is that OK?'

Again, the little girl nodded.

'Ok then. I'm going to start off with a few questions just to get you used to the machine,' said Dr Tabor. 'First of all, what's your name?'

'Samantha Allison Lowe.'

'And where do you live?'

'With my Mummy and Daddy.'

'Do you know the address?'

'Yes. It's 17 Kingsland Park Avenue, Cheadle, Cheshire.'

Unseen by anyone except Dr Tabor, Samantha's eyes remained glued to the moving green light.

'You're doing very well Samantha,' Dr Tabor reassured her.

'Now, when you were very young you were very ill weren't you?'

'Yes.'

'And you had to have an operation didn't you? Can you tell me what that operation was for?'

'They gave me a new heart because mine wasn't working properly. They gave me the heart from another little girl who had died.'

'That's very good Samantha. Now, since you had that operation you've been having some bad dreams haven't you? I want you to tell me all about them please.'

Samantha began: 'I don't like them, they frighten me. I don't want to talk about them.'

Ray sighed to himself. Another wasted exercise. Another waste of his time.

But then, completely unbidden, Samantha continued: 'When they started it was just lights. All colours of lights: red, green, white, orange, blue. All colours. And then I started seeing faces, not proper ones at first, just face shapes but they really frightened me. Then after that, I knew one of the faces was a girl and she was saying something to me but I couldn't tell what she was saying properly. I think it was "Don't" but I couldn't tell.'

Ray, Fairfax and Samantha's parents sat transfixed, not daring to move a muscle in case the slightest movement ruined the moment. She wasn't saying anything she hadn't said before, but all three of them were struck by the calmness in her voice. Inevitably, trying to get her to discuss her nightmares ended in tears and genuine fear. But now she was composed, dispassionate almost, pouring out her heart to a total stranger in scary spectacles.

'When I started to see more, that's when it started to get really spooky,' she went on. 'I knew that I was the other girl. But she wasn't me. She was older than me and she had red hair but mine's blonde. I knew that what was happening to me in my nightmare had happened to her. But everything was all mixed-up in my head. People kept asking me about it but it was all jumbled up and the words wouldn't come out.

'And I knew I — we — were tied up. And I knew we were in a van or something and we were being driven somewhere because all the lights were street lights and traffic lights and stuff.'

Miriam Tabor interrupted. 'Samantha, you're doing really, really well but I just want to ask you something. How did you end up in the van?'

Still following the green lights, the little girl said: 'I got in it.'

'Why did you do that?' asked Dr Tabor gently.

'Because I thought it was my swimming instructor,' she replied. 'The van stopped and the man shouted "Get in, I'll give you a lift." He looked like my swimming instructor so I got in. When he drove off again I realised it wasn't him and that I didn't know who he was but he wouldn't let me out. I started screaming and crying but he hit me and told me to shut up. Then he stopped the van and put some tape over my mouth. Then he dragged me into the back and tied me up.'

Ray realised that what he was listening to was an eye-witness account from the victim of a brutal and sadistic murder; the statement of a dead girl. A statement that appeared to put Robert Craymer in the clear. There wasn't a cat in hell's chance of it being admissible evidence in court, but it might give him a valuable lead.

He mouthed to Miriam Tabor: 'Description.'

She appeared slightly annoyed but asked Samantha: 'Samantha, can you tell me anything about this man? Like what he looked like or what he was wearing?'

'He's big and he's very strong,' the child said, as if describing someone who stood in front of her. 'And he's nearly bald. And he's got a little beardy thing. That's how I knew it wasn't Bob. He hasn't got a beard.'

'Samantha, this is really good,' said Dr Tabor. 'Just tell us who Bob is.'

'He's my swimming instructor. I like him. He's nice. But this man frightened me.'

110

Kate and Peter Lowe exchanged glances of incomprehension. This was their daughter; their only child. Yet here she was, talking as if she was somebody else entirely. Could this be it? Could this really be the beginning of the end to Samantha's problems? Could life really return to normal?

Richard Fairfax allowed himself a feeling of self-justification. To his mind, what he was hearing was proof that the theory of cellular memory was correct. And in that moment, he felt his life change. There would be papers to write for learned medical journals; lectures to deliver and interviews to give; maybe even TV chat shows. He would be known as 'The Doctor Who Proved the Theory of Cellular Memory.' And just as he had hoped, Samantha Lowe would be his White Crow.

Ray's mind was racing through what he now knew. Robert Craymer could no longer be considered a suspect. He had heard the 'dead girl' say it wasn't him driving the van. It was a bald man with a little beard. But who was he? And where did he take her in the van and what happened when they got there? There were more questions he needed Miriam Tabor to ask.

Then, just as suddenly as it had started, it ended.

'I don't want to do anymore,' Samantha announced. 'I'm tired.'

'But...' The protest died unspoken in Ray's throat.

'That's fine sweetheart. You've done really, really well,' Dr Tabor was saying. 'We'll stop right there but I'd like you to come back and talk to me again. Will you do that for me?'

'Yes, alright,' replied Samantha, nervously twisting the ties on her hood.

Ray said, 'Doctor, there's a lot more I need to know. Can't we carry on?'

Dr Tabor fixed him with a look that, had it been a blow, would have knocked him out.

'Chief Inspector, I told you right at the out-set that this process is patient-led,' she said. 'The patient has to want to do it if it's to have any value. You heard Samantha say she doesn't want to do it any more today but that she will come back and talk to me again. We will make her an appointment before she leaves today and that will be the end of the matter.'

Ray pushed on. 'But we all heard what she said. There is obviously information in her head that will be invaluable to helping me catch a murderer. I need to know what else she knows.'

'Mr Wilson, maybe I didn't make myself clear,' said the doctor. 'The answer is no. My priority as a doctor is to help this little girl overcome the trauma that's troubling her. Quite frankly, helping you catch your killer is of secondary importance to me.'

Ray knew when he was beaten. 'Well, do you think you could let me know when her next appointment is?'

Dr Tabor glared at him, the blue tint of her glasses intensifying the blaze in her eyes. 'I don't think that would be appropriate under the circumstances. I will, however, pass on to you anything more she says about the man she began to describe today, along with anything else that may have a bearing on the crimes you're investigating. Now, if you'll excuse me.'

As a dismissal, it was up there with, 'Never darken my doorstep again.' Richard Fairfax and the Lowes didn't move.

'Well, thank you all. It's been very informative,' he said and then, looking directly at Kate Lowe, added, 'I'll be in touch.'

At the bottom of the staircase he found the Sky Scraper Woman sitting behind a highly polished desk that was a miniature version of her boss's. There was a smugness in her tone as, without looking up from her computer keyboard, she said, 'Goodbye Mr Wilson.'

Making his way back to the side street in which he had left his car on a very expensive meter, Ray knew he had been humiliated and treated like a naughty schoolboy by a haughty medic and he fought to control the anger that welled up inside him. Maybe she just didn't like working in front of an audience. Maybe she didn't like coppers. Or maybe she just didn't like men.

The indignation he felt was buoyed by the new information he now had; information that on the face of it did little to help catch the killer yet did appear to clear the prime suspect. But there was a lot more work that needed to be done. The way ahead was not as clear as he had hoped it would be after Samantha's EMDR session. He needed a sign; something, anything that would point him in the right direction.

Then all at once the sign appeared in front of him and he knew exactly what steps to take. The sign said, 'White Lion.'

CHAPTER 16

It had been more than a week since Samantha had her first EMDR session with Dr Tabor and Ray was feeling frustrated. The description Samantha had given would fit thousands of men. Indeed, there were parts of West Yorkshire where a shaved head and goatee were so common they were almost a uniform. And men who chose such an appearance usually had tattoos, sometimes lots of them.

If only Miriam Tabor had carried on with the session a bit longer, Samantha might have come up with something that would have given him a more positive lead. But she hadn't so, as it was, all he had been able to tell his team was that Robert Craymer was no longer in the frame. The reason he gave for reaching that conclusion sounded even crazier to him as he said it than it did when he first heard the words tumble from Samantha's mouth.

The North Sea looked calm and placid, almost inviting, as he drove into Whitby. It was the weekend again and time to relax. Ray was delighted that his renewed interest in sailing had given him an excuse to get away from work and that no one in Whitby Yacht Club was actually much interested in what he did. People who asked were told he was a police officer but nothing more. His new-found friends were much more interested in his sailing experiences, where he had raced, in what kind of boat and who with. None of them had an inkling that he was a senior detective investigating the horrific kidnap, rape and murder of a young girl.

He arrived in the town early Friday evening, checked into the B&B — where, as a regular customer, he now got a preferential rate — then went straight to the yacht club for a snack and a beer.

He had been drinking for an hour or so with a couple of his fellow crewmen and the skipper of another boat when the door opened and a blonde woman walked in. Ray had manoeuvred himself into a position where his back was to the bar and he had an open view of the room, an old habit that had never died.

The new arrival caught his eye the moment she stepped across the threshold and he found himself captivated as she walked straight towards the company at the bar. Her hair was fashionably tousled. Skin tight jeans and stiletto heels showed off her long legs. Ray hadn't taken his eyes off her when she joined the party, slipping her arm through that of the skipper of a rival boat, who Ray knew only as Neil.

The gesture generated mixed feelings of disappointment and relief in Ray. Yes, she was a very attractive woman and no, she wasn't available. Another one. Don't even go there. Just carry on as normal.

'Everyone, this is my baby sister Belle,' Neil was saying.

It took a second to register. Baby sister. So maybe she wasn't attached after all. No, forget it.

But as the evening wore on, he found himself more and more captivated by her piercing blue-grey eyes and her full lips, accentuated by bright red lipstick. It took Ray a while to register that he had seen her before; that she sailed on her brother's boat; that he had raced against her. The difference was, the only times he had seen her previously she had been without make-up, enveloped in functional but unflattering sailing gear, topped off by a lifejacket and a big woolly hat.

They exchanged pleasantries but little more and parted wishing each other good luck for the following day's race. But as Ray walked back to the B&B, he couldn't get her out of his mind.

After the race, Ray followed his usual routine of stripping off his sailing kit, stuffing it back in his battered bag, which he dumped by the club door, and headed for the bar. The 'inquest' with his crewmates about where the day's tactics had gone right or wrong was in full flow when Ray felt a hand on his arm. He turned and found himself face to face with Belle.

'So, you beat us then,' she said. Unlike Ray, she had spent the time since the race ended changing into decent clothes and putting on her make-up. And once more he was captivated.

'Well, we beat you on the water,' answered Ray, 'but I'm not sure we were far enough ahead of you to beat you on handicap,' referring to the complicated system of time correction that, in theory at least, equalised every boat in the race. 'What can I get you to drink?'

Over the next two hours, Ray drifted away from his crewmates and concentrated his attentions on Belle. He found out that Belle was short for Isabelle — 'It just didn't suit me. It's such a feminine name and I was a bit of a tom-boy at school' — and that she worked as a paralegal for a firm of specialist personal injury lawyers in Middlesbrough.

She had been sailing since she was 16 but only started big-boat sailing four years ago when her brother bought his yacht. Her ambition was to race around the world with one of the companies that specialise in providing such adventure for amateur sailors.

Ray managed to tell her little of himself other than he came from Cambridgeshire, that he was currently working as a police officer with the West Yorkshire force and that he lived alone in a cottage on the moors between Bradford and Manchester.

She managed to get out of him that he was actually a Detective Chief Inspector on the Major Incident Team but let that go with nothing more than, 'I bet that's interesting.' To which he simply replied, 'It can be.' And they moved on.

Finally, Belle asked: 'Do you fancy getting something to eat? I'm starving.'

'Sure,' said Ray. 'What's the choice?'

'Well, you can have pretty much whatever you want. But there are a lot of very good fish restaurants — and a couple of really excellent fish and chip restaurants.'

'Fish and chips it is then.'

Without saying goodbye to anybody, the pair of them slipped out of the yacht club. On the way to the restaurant, Belle slipped her arm through Ray's. He reacted nonchalantly to the gesture and attempted not to attach any significance to it, but from deep down inside a feeling of warmth began to creep through him.

Their chosen restaurant was busy when they arrived and they were asked to wait 10 minutes or so for a table to become available. In the end, they waited more than half an hour, but Ray did not complain. He was delighting in Belle's company and he wouldn't have minded if it had taken hours to get a table. He found her witty, charming, intelligent and

— most importantly from his point of view — completely unconnected to his day job.

By the time they were shown to a table for two, they had both had more beer.

Both of them ordered haddock and chips, to which Ray extravagantly added a bottle of champagne. 'Someone once told me it's the only thing to drink with fish and chips,' he said.

'I usually have tea but what the hell,' she replied.

Afterwards, with full stomachs and slightly spinning heads, they headed into town where Belle guided him towards a cocktail bar, a garish, neon-lit, chrome and glass edifice that he would never normally contemplate. But this time, he felt powerless to resist.

A superbly mixed dry martini was followed by a classic Singapore Sling and topped off by a Long Island Iced Tea, at the end of which neither of them was making any sense. They communicated in half-finished sentences, mispronounced words and giggles.

By now, darkness had fallen, the sky was spattered with stars and a full moon cast ghostly shadows over the ruins of St Mary's Church. Belle pulled him close and slurred something in his ear which his brain interpreted as, 'Do you want to come back to mine for a nightcap? It's not far. We can get a cab'

Beyond reasoned thought, he slurred something back which her brain interpreted as, 'Why not.'

Ten minutes later, they were outside a smart terraced house on the outskirts of town. The door had barely closed behind them when they began to rip each other's clothes off with an ardour undimmed by the drink.

The insistent jangling of his mobile phone dragged Ray from his coma-like state. At first his eyes couldn't take in his surroundings. His brain couldn't identify his location. His mouth felt like it had been sandpapered and coated with creosote. Then he felt movement by his side and a glimpse of blonde hair poking above the duvet brought the previous night flooding back.

His phone was still ripping the silence. Where was it? Why hadn't it tripped to answerphone? He rifled through clothes scattered like confetti until he eventually found it, stuffed in the side pocket of his sailing trousers. By now, it had stopped ringing but before he could find out who the missed call was from, the phone emitted the dit-dit-dit, dah-dah, dit-dit-dit — Morse Code for SMS — that indicated he had a text message.

It read, 'Ring me urgently. Jan'.

'I'm sorry to bother you on a Sunday Boss,' said Jan Holroyd as she answered his call. 'But I thought you'd better know that local radio is linking the murders of Kylie Morris and Zoe Clayton.'

She was expecting a stream of invective but instead Ray calmly replied, 'I'm surprised no one's done it sooner. And you never know it might actually help us. Joe Public loves a good serial killer.'

'There is that I suppose,' said Jan. 'I think the info's come from North Yorkshire but it's hard to tell whether it's official or whether it's a leak. The radio mentioned similarities — the girls' ages, how they were killed, and the way their bodies were dumped. But there is a significant difference to our enquiry. They're looking for a blue van.'

'A blue van? But ours is red.'

'Yeah I know. Do you want me to ring North Yorks and find out what that's based on?'

'Good idea. Look, I'm still in Whitby. I'll be there in about three hours. Are you in the office?'

'Yes Boss.'

'OK, I'll see you later.'

He found the bathroom and took a quick shower. He rubbed toothpaste over his teeth using his index finger and then found a bottle of mouthwash, which only added another dimension to the industrial flavours polluting in his mouth.

Belle slept soundly as he dressed and didn't waken when he gently kissed the top of her head.

Downstairs he found paper and a pen and left a note. 'Sorry I had to dash,' it read. 'Duty calls. I'll ring you in the week.'

It would be at least an hour before he realised that not only did he not have either a mobile or a landline number for Belle, he couldn't even remember her last name.

In his Bradford hovel, the radio had been nothing more than background while he leafed through his favourite Sunday tabloid — until he heard the names Kylie Morris and Zoe Clayton. He missed most of what was said but the mere mention of both girls' names was enough to send his heart rate soaring.

He spent an anxious hour wondering what the police had discovered as he waited for the news to be repeated. What he heard sent his pulse racing to the point he could feel the blood pumping in his temples.

Detectives investigating the murder of Zoe Clayton were searching for a small, blue, square-shaped van and had linked her killing to that of schoolgirl Kylie Morris...

The rest was lost in a blur as his mind tumbled over itself as he struggled to make sense of what he had just heard.

Someone had seen him, of that there could be no doubt. Despite all his care to be discreet he, or rather the van, had been seen. But how had they linked his van to the girl? He must have been seen near the swimming pool or maybe...

The details didn't matter, he decided. What was important now was to get rid of the van.

He didn't even consider his options; didn't give a thought to the pros and cons of the various ways he could destroy all links with the vehicle. It would have to be crushed.

Once it was a small cube of metal, he believed, PC Plod wouldn't have a cat in hell's chance of recovering even the tiniest scrap of useful information from it. All he had to do was put the right registration plates back on and take it to a scrapyard somewhere far away. But his twisted logic told him not to go North. Plod would be watching in the North.

Early next morning he drove onto the M62, heading east towards Hull and then joined the M1 southbound, heading somewhere he hadn't yet decided. The signposts flashed by: Wakefield, Barnsley, Rotherham, Sheffield, Chesterfield, Mansfield, Nottingham.

Nottingham. It attracted him. He would never be able to explain why; it just felt like the right place. And he knew it would be big enough to have a station where he could get a train home. He turned off the motorway and followed the signs for the city centre. It was a place he had never been before and he was totally lost, so he just kept on driving.

Aimless, clueless, a motorised drifter in a strange new world, his heart leapt for joy when he stopped at a set of traffic lights. There, directly in front of him, was a scrap merchant's lorry, its giant skip full to the brim with twisted, rusting metal. So he took a gamble and followed it.

Twenty minutes later, after crossing the city centre, the lorry — with its unofficial escort — had entered an area that was in industrial decline. Run-down lock-ups sat alongside open forecourts that offered hand car washes for £3. The streets were getting narrower and narrower when the lorry suddenly indicated a right turn. And there it was. A scrap yard, piled high with abandoned, wrecked, broken and unloved cars and vans.

By one of those quirks of fate, the scrapyard owner was not on the premises when the blue van turned up to ends its days. He was on his way back from Leeds, where he had spent the weekend visiting his in-laws.

When he finally arrived, late in the afternoon, the van, minus its wheels, was sitting in a line of other wrecks waiting to be cannibalised before being dropped into the crusher. He made a bee-line for the office and his son, who he had left in charge.

There were no niceties. 'Where the fuck's that blue van come from?' was his opening shot.

'What blue van?' answered his startled son, hastily swinging his legs off the desk.

'The only blue van out there. The one that's waiting for the crusher.'

'Oh yeah, that one. Some bloke brought it in this morning.'

'Did you get his name?'

'Course I did,' said the youth. 'I'm not stupid.'

'Show me.'

The lad rummaged around the papers littering the desk until he found the registration book in which the name and address of everybody from whom the yard bought scrap metal was supposed to be logged.

He flicked it open and stabbed a grimy finger at the last entry. 'There.'

His father scanned the entry then hurled the book back at him.

'Robin Hood? 72 Sherwood Forest Avenue?' he yelled. 'Was he carrying a fuckin' bow and arrow as well? You stupid tosser.'

The lad was quick to his own defence. 'How do you know that's not his real name and address? It could be.'

'Think about it you prick. Which city are we in?

'Er Nottingham.'

'Exactly. Nottingham. Famous for? Robin Hood and his merry fuckin' men that's who. Sherwood Forest. Maid Marian. Friar Tuck. Ring any bells?'

'Er, oh yeah, like...I geddit now. Anyway, what's the big deal? We can get some good parts of it. It's a runner.'

'I'll tell you what the big deal is, cock. While I was in Leeds there was a story on the radio about some fuckin' pervert who's raped and murdered two little girls. And he drives a blue van. Bit of a coincidence don't you think?'

The youth looked suitably chastened. 'Sorry Dad. I gave a hundred quid for it. I thought we could get three or four times that back. I didn't know did I?'

The incident room running the inquiry into Zoe Clayton's murder had been quiet all day and now, as the clock ticked round to 5.30pm, Detective Sergeant Frank Cartwright was looking forward to a couple of pints on his way home. Then the phone rang.

'Oh, hello,' said a hesitant voice. 'My name's Whiteside. Brian Whiteside. I run a scrapyard in Nottingham. The thing is, I've been in Leeds for the weekend...'

Frank Cartwright stifled a yawn.

'And I heard on the radio about you're looking for a small blue van. Well, when I got back to work just now...'

Frank Cartwright resisted the urge to tell the caller to get on with it.

'There's one in the yard. My son bought it off a bloke this morning.'

Frank Cartwright was suddenly very interested. 'Say that again. You've got a small blue van that was scrapped just this morning?'

'Yeah. It's a Ford Transit Connect.'

'And it's blue? What shade of blue?'

'Er, it's dark blue. At least on the outside it is.'

'What do you mean, on the outside it is?'

'It's been resprayed and badly too. It's red inside.'

'You've got a name and address for the man who sold it?'

'Well, yeah. But I'm pretty certain it's not his real name.'

'Why not?'

'He said he was called Robin Hood. And he gave his address as Sherwood Forest Avenue.'

Frank Cartwright became authoritative. 'Right Mr Whiteside, this is what I need you to do. Make sure no one touches the vehicle or goes anywhere near it. Don't do anything to it. I'll arrange for someone to come and have a look at it and collect it. In the meantime, don't mention it to anybody.'

'Can I carry on with the business?' asked Whiteside.

'Not until we've taken the vehicle away. Now, what's the address?'

Fuckin' great, Whiteside thought as he gave the yard's address. You try to help and finish up with the bastards not letting you work.

As it happened, Brian Whiteside had no real cause for concern about lost business. By 8.30am the next morning, a low-loader had arrived to take the van. With the low-loader were two forensic scientists to ensure there was no chance of further contamination of the van. Whiteside and his son were fingerprinted for elimination purposes, even though Whiteside said he hadn't touched the van and his son claimed only to have removed the wheels.

By early afternoon the van was locked away in a secure unit at the North Yorkshire Police HQ in Northallerton. It looked like something from a sci-fi film. The protective shield of thick plastic sheeting that had been erected around it gave off an eerie glow from the high-intensity arc lights inside that bathed the van in brilliant white light. Five boffins, identically dressed in all-enveloping, hooded white suits with surgical face masks and safety glasses, poured over every square inch.

As he watched, Ray felt his stomach rumble. He'd missed lunch again, even though he had known the previous night that he would need to be in Northallerton that afternoon. Alongside him DCI Paul Connors, his counterpart from North Yorkshire CID, called out, 'Anything to tell us yet Jill?'

One of the scientists stopped work and walked towards them, pushing back the hood of the protective suit, shaking loose a mop of auburn hair and lowering her face mask as she did so.

'We've only done a preliminary examination at the moment,' she explained. 'We'll be getting on to the deep search stuff soon but right now it's not looking promising. There's nothing obvious. If this is the van you're looking for I think someone may have given it a good clean.'

Ray said, 'I'd be very interested to know if you find anything that looks like cat hair.'

The woman threw him a quizzical look before Connors got in. 'Sorry. I haven't introduced you two. This is DCI Ray Wilson. He's heading up the investigation into Kylie Morris's murder. And this is Jill Thornton, Doctor Jill Thornton. She's in charge of this facility.'

'Did you say cat hair?' she asked, a puzzled expression on her face.

'Yes I did,' said Ray. 'I know it sounds odd but both girls had cat hair on their bodies. We had a prime suspect who lives in a house full of the bloody things but none of them matched the hairs found on the bodies. If there are any in the van I'd be interested to know if they match the ones we've found already. It could help prove the girls were in the van.'

'Aha. The old Meowplex Test eh?' smiled Thornton.

'So you're familiar with the test?' asked Ray.

'I wouldn't say familiar. I know about it but I've never used it. Still, first time for everything and all that.'

The voice Ray heard when he answered his office telephone two days later was not the one he expected. It was a voice cracked by emotion, fractured by fear. But he knew immediately who it belonged to.

'Ray. She's gone. She's gone. You have to find her. Help me, please.' Kate Lowe was hysterical and he didn't have to ask any questions to understand why. Samantha, her vulnerable, fragile daughter, was missing and Kate's mind was running through every one of the unspeakable fates that could have befallen her.

CHAPTER 17

It took Ray several minutes to calm Kate down enough for her to be able to tell him what had happened. That morning she had dropped Kate off at the school gates as usual and then driven the three miles into Stockport and her part-time job. Ninety minutes later, the school rang her to ask if Kate was ill because she wasn't in class — and the nightmare began.

He could hear her sobbing down the phone as she pleaded, 'What's happened to her Ray? Where is she? I just want her back.'

Ray had the urge to drive to Manchester and hold her; hold her close until the world was alright again. Instead, his professionalism took over.

'Kate, have you reported Samantha missing to your local police?' She hadn't.

'Does Peter know what's happened?' He didn't.

'Look Kate, I know this is difficult for you, especially given Samantha's issues, but you need to ring the police straight away. I'll put a call in from here explaining her involvement in our murder inquiries. Ring Peter and tell him what's happened, then go home and wait for the police. Dig out the best photograph of Samantha you can find.'

'A photograph? What for?'

'It's just routine,' he said calmly. 'They'll give it to all their patrols, just in case she's wandering the streets. And they may issue it to the media, if they think it would help.'

'Oh Ray. What if...' Kate was beginning to fall apart again.

'Don't even go there,' he replied. 'All we know for certain is that she isn't in school. Try not to think about what ifs. The police in Greater Manchester will do their level best to find her. And if you need someone to talk to, you can call me any time, day or night. You know that don't you?'

There was a barely audible, 'Yes. Thanks Ray,' before she hung up.

He saw her purely by chance. A glimpse of blonde hair, a tiny figure in a landscape of adults towering around her. But the bonus was none of them appeared to be with her. She was alone.

He hadn't left home with the intention of doing it again, but with the sight of the girl's blonde hair and that fact she was available, the urge crashed over him with the power of an ocean wave. Plus he was in Manchester, well away from his previous hunting grounds and he had a new van. Well, it was new to him, even though it looked like it was coming to the end of its useful life and carried the scars and dents to show just how hard it had been worked. And just in case any nosey parker did think he was acting suspiciously, the number plates his mate in the trade had made up for him without questioning the reason why, matched to a bus he had seen in Leeds.

Now, suddenly, she had gone; swallowed up by the crowd and the cars and the cabs swirling around the station. A hastily executed U-turn brought the blaring wrath of car horns but he didn't care. He was hunting.

Not knowing whether the girl had just arrived at the station or was planning to go inside it, he made a couple of passes before he spotted her again. She looked a bit younger than the other two, but looks could be deceptive couldn't they? It could have been the school uniform that knocked a couple of years off her. And she seemed a bit smaller, not that that mattered.

What was the same was the ease with which he tempted her into his van.

He pulled up alongside her, wound down the window and said, 'Hiya sugar. Your Mum said I might find you here. Do you want a lift?'

Unquestioning, she nodded and climbed into the passenger seat. It was that simple. Whatever did they teach them in school these days? Did modern kids know nothing about Stranger Danger?

He could see she was only about 10, too young to be out alone in a big city. But now she wasn't alone. She was with him. And the creaking van's still-operative central locking system ensured that was where she would stay. He would drive out of the city centre, find somewhere he could bind and gag her unseen and then take her to the usual place, where the fun would begin. The very thought of it began to get him excited.

The local radio stations began carrying the news of Samantha's disappearance in their mid-afternoon news bulletins. They gave a description and the fact that she was wearing her school uniform. The official line from the police was that they were 'concerned for her welfare' and wanted anybody who thought they may have seen her to come forward. By teatime, the two regional television stations in the city were preparing to use the picture of Samantha issued by the Greater Manchester Police Press Office. It was the picture that her mother had chosen to hand over. But the picture showed a girl with long blonde hair cascading over her shoulders, wearing her favourite pink track suit, which was a wholly different image from that of the eight year-old who had left home for school that morning.

Apart from the call from Kate Lowe, Ray had had another uneventful day. There had been no word from the forensics team about the van; no word from them either about whether they had found any cat hairs and public apathy was overwhelming. He was toying with the idea of taking his team for a pint when one of them shouted through to him, 'Boss, I've got GMP on the 'phone asking for you.'

The caller introduced himself as Superintendent Norman Marr. He said he was calling from Stockport police station where he was in charge of the search for Samantha Lowe. 'I believe you have some kind of relationship with Mrs Lowe, is that correct?' asked Marr. A relationship. He wished. He knew it could never be and should never be. But deep down...

'I wouldn't exactly call it a relationship, sir,' said Ray, with due deference to the higher rank. 'I know Mr and Mrs Lowe — and Samantha too — on a professional basis. I have reason to believe that Samantha is key to an on-going enquiry we are conducting.'

'Sorry Mr Wilson, I wasn't implying anything improper,' stumbled Marr. 'It's just that Mrs Lowe has suddenly decided she won't speak to anybody but you. Bit frustrating, as I'm sure you'll agree. We're doing our best to find her little girl and then she turns round and says she'll only speak to someone from another force and won't even tell us why.'

'I can understand your frustration,' replied Ray, 'but Samantha is not like other little girls. I'm not going to go into details but suffice it to say she's different. And, of course, I'll do anything I can to help.'

'Can you get over here? Now?'

Ray glanced at his watch. Just before 5.30pm. The traffic would be heavy and frustratingly slow-moving for a man who had to be 45 miles away as quickly as possible. He could always get a traffic patrol to blue-light it all the way to Stockport but there would be hell to pay when his bosses found out.

'Yes sir. I'll leave right away. Be with you as quickly as I can.'

The clock behind Stockport police station's reception desk had just ticked past 7.0pm when Ray introduced himself and asked for Superintendent Marr.

The female civilian support staff member who greeted him picked up a telephone, dialled a three digit extension and announced his arrival. All she said was, 'Yes sir. Right away.' She then disappeared through a door and reappeared seconds later at Ray's side. 'Please follow me Mr Wilson,' she said, turning left into a corridor that ran off the reception area at right angles. They passed several offices, Ray's rubber-soled shoes making squeaking sounds on the parquet flooring. After about 30 yards and approaching the end of the 1960s building, they came face-to-face with a door on which a brass plaque announced: Supt N. Marr. She knocked on the door and waited until a voice on the other side boomed, 'Come in.' She ushered Ray through the door and stepped back into the corridor, closing it behind her.

Norman Marr was a bear of a man. He stood almost 6' 5" tall and weighed in the region of 18st but without a suspicion of fat, even though he was in his mid-40s. The thought occurred to Ray that 20 years previously this man would have made a formidable rugby forward. Marr stood to greet him but before he could take the outstretched hand, Kate Lowe jumped up from the chair opposite Marr's desk and launched herself at Ray, throwing her arms around his neck and kissing him on the cheek. Ray was visibly staggered, confused and surprised by her greeting. Gone was the normal reserve; gone was her apparent indifference towards him; gone was her apparent shyness. In that instant Marr could have been forgiven for thinking that perhaps his inappropriate remark to Ray that he had a "relationship" with Mrs Lowe wasn't that far wide of the mark after all. Of Peter Lowe, there was no sign.

'Oh Ray, Ray. Thank you for coming,' gushed Kate. 'I'm so pleased to see you. I can't tell you how much it means to me.' A second later the façade collapsed. Her bottom lip began to quiver, her face crumpled and tears welled in her eyes. 'She's gone Ray. She's gone,' she sobbed. 'They can't find her Ray. I just know something's wrong. I knew it when she was born and I know it now. I've always known. Ray, what can we do?'

Ray was very conscious that he hadn't yet formally introduced himself to Norman Marr. 'Kate, the first thing we need to do is tell Mr Marr every little thing we can about Samantha. About the transplant and the problems that followed and about what the doctors think. Come on, let's sit down.'

A handshake dispensed with the formalities, Marr ordered tea for the three of them and then spent the next hour listening as Kate, helped by Ray, went through Samantha's life story.

Ray could see that Marr was struggling with the concept of cellular memory and was reminded of his own difficulties grasping the notion that memory could be preserved in any organ of the body. He had just embarked on his layman's explanation when Marr held up a giant right hand as if he was bringing a line of traffic to a halt. 'Mr Wilson, it's enough for me to know that you and Mrs Lowe believe this theory,' he said. 'I don't need to understand it. I think what we really need to explore are the facets of Samantha's life that might have — how can I put this? — persuaded her to leave home and where those thoughts might have taken her.'

A brief flash of anger crossed Kate's face. 'How can you be sure she's run away? How do you know she hasn't been abducted or something? She could be dead for all you know.' Tears once again flooded her eyes and her shoulders dropped as she began to sob.

'You're quite right Mrs Lowe,' said Marr. 'We don't know what's happened, but in the absence of any other evidence, I'm taking the optimistic view and that is, something in her life has triggered the flight response. Something has happened that has convinced her young mind that she needs to run to somewhere. Or to someone. And I need you to help me discover what that something is.'

A silence fell on the office, which was large but functional, almost Spartan, except for a framed photograph on Marr's desk of a woman and two boys, who Ray presumed was his family. There was no atmosphere, no awkwardness. It was as if the very life had been sucked from the room, leaving the three occupants frozen in time.

And then Ray was aware that Kate had begun speaking.

'I remember she was very upset by the fact that Kylie Morris had been murdered,' she was saying. 'And she still gets very distressed by her nightmares. Like the doctors say, it's like she's experiencing what poor Kylie went through. She keeps saying she wants to help her but she knows she can't because it's too late. She was so pleased when me and Pete told Tracey and Frank — that's Kylie's mum and dad — that we'd do anything we could to help find whoever killed Kylie. She kept asking what she could do to help and we told her just talking to the doctors and to Ray was enough.'

Both men picked up the clue at the same time, but it was Ray who got the first question in.

'Kate, has Samantha ever met the Morris's?'

'No. But she keeps asking us to take her to meet them,' she replied. 'We thought it best not to take her because it might be too upsetting for her, not to mention the Morris's.'

'They live in Bradford, is that right?' asked Marr.

Before he got an answer, Marr was on the telephone barking orders. 'I want all the CCTV from the railway station, Piccadilly Station and Victoria, as well as the bus station and the ones in Manchester too. And get someone onto the motorway service areas between here and Leeds. I want whatever CCTV they've got from the last 24 hours. Forecourt, shops, car parks, whatever they've got. And I want it now. We're looking for a little girl in school uniform.'

As he put the phone down Marr realised Ray was on his mobile making the same demands of his team in Bradford. 'And Jan, get somebody round to the Morris's just in case Samantha turns up,' he said. 'I don't think she knows their address but if she's smart enough to get herself to Bradford, she's smart enough to find them.'

Just then there was a knock on the door and a civilian support worker entered unbidden, carrying a tray on which were three mugs of tea and a plate of biscuits. She placed them on Marr's desk, saying: 'We thought you could probably do with these sir,' before leaving.

Marr proffered the tray to Kate and then Ray, who put the mug to his lips and then, feeling the heat radiating from it, thought better of it and put it down. He took the opportunity to ask the question that had remained unasked since he first arrived. 'Kate, where's Peter?'

'He's out in a patrol car with a couple of my lads,' Marr replied for her. 'It's a bit a needle in a haystack job I know, but they're trawling the streets, just in case she's still in town.'

They drank the tea, each lost in their own thoughts, not a word passing between them, just like old friends. Except they barely knew each other and none had an inkling what the other two were thinking. Eventually, Marr drained his mug and put it back on the tray. 'Mrs Lowe, I don't think there's anything constructive to be gained by you staying here,' he said. 'I'm quite happy for you to go home. I'll make sure your husband knows where you are. Would you like me to get you a car?'

Ray answered for her. 'That's OK sir. I'll take Mrs Lowe home. It's on my way back to the motorway.'

Only if you're hopelessly lost, thought Marr. 'Fine. We'll obviously keep in touch and if there are any developments we'll let you know Mrs Lowe. You too, Chief Inspector.'

Minutes later, they were alone in Ray's car, heading for a deserted house where they would still be alone. Ray's mind was racing. This shouldn't be. He shouldn't be here with this woman; this woman who was a significant part of a major investigation he was conducting; this woman who was frightened to death for the safety of her young daughter; this woman who was the doppelganger of the dead woman who had been the love of his life.

Apart from Kate giving directions, the journey passed in silence. When they arrived at the house, she calmly asked if he would like coffee. He knew he should say no, but in the turmoil that was his mind at that moment, he heard himself saying it would be lovely. As she turned the key in the lock, Ray caught the aroma of her perfume, familiar but somehow unplaceable and yet strangely comforting. She hung her coat on the banister and carried on into the sizeable, square kitchen that was immediately off the hall, Ray following her like a lap-dog.

He watched as she filled the electric kettle and put ground coffee beans into a cafetiere. Then she reached up to retrieve two china mugs from a cupboard, her blouse riding up to momentarily reveal her well-toned stomach. Once again Ray was filled with the urge to pull her close, embrace her and tell her everything would be alright. But he knew that if he did that everything would be far from alright. At best she would slap him hard and he would lose potentially the best chance he had of catching a killer. At worst, she would report him and he would stand a fair chance of being sacked.

The shrill tone of his mobile snapped him back into the real world.

It was Supt Marr. 'Mr Wilson, are you still with Mrs Lowe?' he asked.

'Yes sir,' he replied, sensing this wasn't just a social call.

'Well, can you bring her back here straight away? We've found something I need to her to look at.'

Ray glanced at Kate, who was focused on preparing the coffee, pouring cream — not milk, he noticed — into a small china jug, as if it was something she had to do to occupy her mind. And he had the feeling her life was about to be irretrievably shattered.

'Yes sir. Straight away.'

By the time they reached the police station Kate was a quivering wreck, dark streaks of eye make-up marking her cheeks with the paths of her tears. Her mind refused to grasp what Ray had told her; couldn't understand why he didn't know the answers to the questions she kept spitting at him. Inside, Supt Marr was already waiting for them at the reception desk, an equally distraught Peter Lowe by his side. Kate fell on him like a demolished tower-block.

'Mrs Lowe, would the two of you come with me?' was all he said. 'And you'd better come to Wilson.'

The four of them took the corridor towards Marr's office. Outside the door he stopped and turning to the Lowe's explained, 'Before we go in, you need to know that we've found a school uniform and I need you to have a look at it and tell me whether you recognise it.'

'No. No. I can't.' The wail came from deep inside Kate. 'Please no. Don't make me. Pete, help me.'

The two senior policemen glanced at each other. They had both seen this reaction before. Parents faced with the task of identifying an object that would confirm their worst fears was a pitiable sight. But it was something that had to be done.

Peter Lowe suddenly seemed gripped by a hidden strength. He stood erect, assured, in command. 'Kate, sweetheart, we have to do this. We have to do this together,' he said gently. 'I'll be with you. We'll be there for each other. But we have to see. Come on. Come with me.'

He slipped his arm around his wife's shoulders as, sobbing loudly but without protest, she walked with him through the door Supt Marr was holding open from the inside.

Laid out on a table that Marr obviously used for meetings were four evidence bags containing a white polo shirt, a blue sweatshirt, complete with a school badge, a grey pleated skirt and a small pink rucksack. The clothes, clean and with no apparent stains, looked pathetically small.

At the sight of what was before her, Kate's knees buckled and she emitted a cry, half strangled by emotion that sounded like 'Nooo.' By her side, Peter's face crumpled into a flood of tears as he struggled to keep his collapsing wife on her feet, steering her towards a hard-backed chair proffered by Ray.

It was a heart-breaking scene but Marr needed confirmation, no matter how difficult.

'Mrs Lowe,' he began, but got no further.

'It's not hers,' Kate managed through the sobs and sniffles. 'It's not Samantha's.'

For a millisecond a quizzical look played across Marr's face. 'Are you quite sure?' he asked.

'Positive,' Kate replied, beginning to recover her composure. 'That uniform's blue but Samantha's is green. Dark green. It's not hers.'

'But...' Whatever Norman Marr was going to say was stifled on his lips by Peter Lowe.

'She's just told you and I'm telling you again. Those things don't belong to Samantha. Now, if you don't mind, I'm going to take her home. She needs rest.'

As the pair of them hobbled towards the door, crippled by heartache, stooped by pain, the giant policeman managed a totally inadequate, 'Thank you for your time. We'll be in touch.'

'Where did this stuff come from?' asked Ray, waving a hand over the exhibits on the table, as they listened to the Lowes progressing down the corridor.

'Birch services on the M62,' replied Marr. 'After we'd been to collect what CCTV footage exists, the duty manager took it upon himself to have a nosy round and found the rucksack in a bin on the eastbound side.

He opened the bag but had the good sense not to touch anything once he saw what was inside.'

'The problem we've got now is if this stuff isn't Samantha's, whose is it? You don't have to be a genius to work out we're probably dealing with another missing child.'

Now he'd got her where he wanted her. Safely hidden away from prying eyes and out of ear-shot, this was his place. His place where could do the things he had discovered sent a thrill of climactic intensity through his body; a thrill much better than any Class A drug he had ever tried; much better than any of the pornographic movies in his secret stash and much better than the whores in the city centre, even the ones who would do anything for cash.

Of course, it was never meant to be like this. He killed the first one in a fit of temper but after it was over, he discovered he'd enjoyed it. The second one was planned because he'd got the urge and that one gave him so much pleasure he did not have the words to describe it. This third one, well, she wasn't planned. She was almost handed to him on a plate, so to speak. She was a bit younger than his others but never look a gift horse in the mouth and all that eh? She'd kicked off a bit when he'd parked up and taken her school uniform off, but a quick slap and some gaffer tape soon sorted that out. Looking back, it was probably not a good idea to dump her uniform in a bin at a motorway service area but with luck, the bin's contents would just get skipped without anyone seeing what's inside.

But he could wait. Anyway, she was sleeping now, thanks largely to the crushed up sleeping pills he had fed her. He had taken off the gaffer tape gag because he didn't want to risk her choking and there was no one around to hear her even if she did wake up and start screaming, but he left her tied up just in case.

Just in case of what, he wasn't exactly certain, but it's what they did on the telly and in the films wasn't it?

And tomorrow, his entertainment could start. It was show time.

CHAPTER 18

On the other side of Manchester, fourteen miles away from where the Lowes had gone through the trauma of having to say whether a young girl's clothes belonged to their daughter or not, another family was living through the nightmare of a missing child. At that moment, Bernard and Christine Docherty were explaining to two young policewomen what they knew about little Anne-Marie's disappearance. She had gone off to the nearby school that morning, bright and cheerful as usual, wearing her uniform of a white polo shirt, blue sweat shirt and a grey, pleated skirt. She'd been carrying a little pink rucksack that contained a small, battered-but-cuddly white rabbit she refused to be separated from and a packet of crisps.

Life on the Ordsall estate in Salford was hard. Christine worked as a cleaner in a four-star hotel on the nearby Salford Quays tourist trap, but Bernard had been out of work for three years. Jobs of any kind were scarce, especially for someone who'd done time for burglary, and the state benefits didn't go very far. Even with Christine's wages it was sometimes hard to put food on the table every single day. And the little treats like cinema trips that better off folk took for granted were a non-starter.

To make matters worse, Christine's ageing dad, Billy Frayn, lived with them. Billy had spent his entire life in Ordsall. He remembered it when it was a warren of terraced streets and never stopped going on about how there used to be a real community spirit; how people used to look after each other and how you never needed to lock your front door. There was none of this drug dealing in his day; none of this vandalism and certainly none of this casual violence. Billy had been a docker when Manchester Docks had been one of the busiest ports in the country, but an accident unloading one of the early container ships meant he lost his right leg just above the knee and he'd never worked since.

The policewomen patiently listened to all this as they tried to get something tangible from the distraught Docherty's. They had a good description — about four feet tall, shoulder length blonde hair, no distinguishing features or marks — and that in addition to her school uniform she was wearing white knee-length socks and black imitation leather trainers with Velcro fastenings.

The school had alerted Christine Docherty that Anne-Marie was missing just after lunch but the family did not report the fact to the police immediately, a symptom of living on the Ordsall estate, where the police were seen as the enemy and anyone who spoke to them was branded a grass. Instead, they tried to find her themselves. Only when that failed did they turn for help.

Their reluctance meant the police were playing catch-up from the very start and it took several hours for them to piece together the start of the trail.

Anne-Marie harboured a secret desire but, unlike other girls of her age, it wasn't to be a pop star or to win the heart of a prince. It wasn't even to visit Disneyland or swim with a dolphin. All she wanted to do was explore Manchester. Even though the city centre was less than four miles from their home, the Docherty's very rarely paid it a visit and when they did, they didn't linger. But to 10 year-old Anne-Marie it was a magical place; a place of towering buildings, giant shops, wide streets bustling with more people than she'd ever seen in her life and more traffic than she could imagine was possible. She was enchanted and had promised herself that one day she would go there on her own. And on that fateful day, that's exactly what she set out to do.

Morning lessons had been boring so, when lunchtime came, she picked up her rucksack and simply walked out of school, unseen and unmissed until the afternoon roll-call. She made her way off the estate, across the busy main road and literally entered another world — the world of Salford Quays with its dozens of luxury apartment developments, bars, restaurants, office buildings and regenerated docks. CCTV would capture her waiting at a Metro tram stop, then, without buying a ticket at the slot machine, boarding a tram heading for the city centre. Even though the tram was virtually empty at this stage of its journey, she chose to sit in one of the four seats located where the two carriages articulated, seats with limited views that many adults found uncomfortable to ride in because of the swinging motion they generated. But just the ticket for a little girl on a big adventure.

She got off the tram in St Peter's Square and began walking. She had no idea where she was and no idea where she was going, but she just kept on walking. Images from street surveillance cameras would later show her walking along Mosley Street, lingering by the fountains in Piccadilly Gardens and then heading off in the direction of Piccadilly Station. It was when she reached the station, she realised that she was lost and didn't know how to get home. She wandered around aimlessly, on the verge of tears, beginning to panic about how she would get home.

And then a man in a van stopped and told her that her Mum had said he would probably find her here.

Ray read the e-mail from Greater Manchester Police with a heavy heart. Another blonde school girl was missing. He already knew that whoever killed Kylie Morris also killed Zoe Clayton. Was this one going to be number three? Maybe they would get lucky and this one really had only run away. But deep down inside he knew differently. After all, he was there when Supt Norman Marr displayed a school uniform that his instincts now told him could only belong to Anne-Marie Docherty. Although no one was saying it out loud, he and all the Manchester coppers working on the poor girl's disappearance were thinking the same thing. It would take a bloody miracle for her to be found alive.

He began to consider whether to bring in a psychological profiler or whether there was anything more useful to be gained from using a geographical profiler first to try and identify the potential area where the killer lived. Or whether to bring both at the same time. And whatever he did, who was going to pay for it? His budget was drum tight and he guessed it would be the same with his colleagues in North Yorkshire and Greater Manchester. He was thinking how wrong it was that cut-backs could affect serious criminal investigations when his lap-top gave the ping that signalled the arrival of a new e-mail. Clicking it open, he didn't immediately recognise the sender's address, but the contents of the message cleared up the puzzle.

It read, 'Full forensic report is in the post but ring me – I've got something you need to know' and was simply signed 'Jill' followed by a mobile number.

Dr Jill Thornton answered her phone on the second ring. After a brief exchange of pleasantries, Ray asked, 'So, have you got some good news for me about cat hairs?'

'Er, yes,' she replied. 'But I've got quite a bit more too.'

She continued, 'The van had been given a good cleaning inside and out before whoever it was sold it for scrap. But they hadn't done a thorough job and left stuff behind. We found cat hairs, like you thought we might. We did the Meowplex test and I can confirm they match the cat hairs from the dead girls' bodies.'

'At least that establishes a link to whoever owns the vehicle then,' said Ray.

'Hang on a minute. There's more,' said the scientist. 'We also found traces of a white fluid that had soaked into the carpet.'

'Dirty bastard,' Ray blurted.

'No, no. It's not what you think. When we tested it, it turned out to be an oil and water emulsion — the kind of stuff that's used in engineering works as a cutting fluid. Looks a bit like milk but has a distinctive smell. From its position on the driver's side floor, I'd say it came from his boots. It's a good bet that the man you're looking for has some connection with the engineering industry.'

'You're quite sure it's a man we're looking for then?' asked Ray.

'Oh yes. No doubt,' she replied. 'I've saved the best bit for last. We've also got his DNA — and a partial thumb print we found on the underside of the driver's door mirror. It's one of the places they always forget to clean.'

Ray was stunned. It was better news than he could ever have hoped for. When he had first met Jill Thornton as she was beginning her investigation of the van, she had primed him to think there wouldn't be much of value to reveal. And now here she was calmly telling him that she had found DNA and a fingerprint that were unlikely to belong to anyone else but the killer.

'How did you get his DNA? When you said the van had been cleaned I thought there'd be no chance of that.'

'Yes, but remember the van hadn't been expertly cleaned. We found a tiny fragment of fingernail embedded into the carpet. It's not much at all but big enough to sample his DNA. And to tell us that whoever he is, he bites his nails.'

There were a few seconds of silence before he said, 'Jill, if you were here right now I think I'd have to kiss you.'

'Whoa, easy tiger. I haven't finished yet,' she said. 'We've also got a partial match on the DNA. The mitochondrial DNA is a match with your person of interest, Robert Craymer.'

Again, there was silence while the implications of what he had just been told sank in.

'Are you telling me he's got a brother?'

'Half-brother. Mitochondrial DNA is inherited from the mother. Craymer and your man have the same mother but different fathers.'

Ray could feel the blood pounding in his temples, his excitement levels rising. This was it. The break through he'd been waiting and hoping for. He tried to retain his composure by asking, 'Have you told DCI Connors about this yet?'

'No, but I will do,' the scientist replied. 'I sent him the same e-mail. You just got to me first.'

'OK. I'm sure I don't have to tell you this but what you've just told me could well turn out to be the turning point in this investigation. I'm indebted to you.'

'No need to be Chief Inspector. It's what we do.'

The telephone had barely hit the rest when Ray yelled through his open office door, 'Jan, Blakey. Get in here now.'

The pair of them hovered in the doorway, Mark Blake still holding a half-eaten bacon sandwich, even though, technically, breakfast time was hours behind them.

'What's up guv?' asked Jan Holroyd.

A half smile played across Ray's lips. At last, he had some good news.

'I've just spoken to the lead forensic investigator working on the van. I want you go and arrest Robert Craymer.'

Blake's brow wrinkled in incredulity. 'Arrest him? What for? I thought he was in the clear.'

'No doubt so did he,' said Ray. 'But I think suspicion of conspiracy to murder might wipe the smile from his face.'

Jan Holroyd's big brown eyes widened to the size of plates. 'Sometimes I fucking love my job,' she said.

They found Robert Craymer at work at the swimming pool. He was in the small area directly alongside the pool that doubled as a reception desk and office, rocked back in a chair, his feet nonchalantly crossed on the desktop as he chatted animatedly to the two young women teachers who accompanied the 30 schoolchildren having swimming lessons. Even though he wasn't actively involved in the lessons, he was dressed in the yellow shorts and polo shirt that was uniform for all pool staff.

He stared at the two police officers with thinly disguised contempt and with one eye on the two teachers, sneered, 'What do you pair of losers want? You know I haven't done anything.'

Holroyd and Blake looked at each other. Jan shrugged and decided that, given this display of arrogance, the direct approach was best.

'Robert Craymer, I am arresting you on suspicion of conspiracy to murder. You do not have to say anything but it may harm your defence if you do not mention when questioned something you later rely on in court. Anything you do say may be given in evidence.'

The arrogance fell from him faster than a brick from a 10-story building.

'What the fuck? You're wrong,' he cried, leaping to his feet. 'You know it's not me. I haven't done anything.'

But before he'd finished his rant, Blake was behind him handcuffing his wrists together.

'Shit. What're doing? Can't I get dressed first?'

Unmoved, Jan snapped, 'No,' as the two teachers looked on with expressions of bemused incomprehension on their faces, witnesses to an act both of them had only ever seen on film. As Blake pushed the stumbling prisoner out on to the pool side, Jan turned to them and said, 'Sorry about that ladies.'

'What's he done?' asked the younger of the two.

'Sorry, I can't tell you that,' Jan replied crisply.

One of the two lifeguards on duty by the pool also saw Craymer being led away.

'Bob, Bob. What's going on?' he yelled across the water, which was giving off the strong, sharp smell that indicates the chlorine has found unwanted organisms to deal with.

'I've been fucking nicked,' was all Craymer could manage before he found himself outside in the street, being invited to mind his head as he was pushed, none too gently, into the back of an unmarked police car. Blake climbed in beside him with a demeanour that suggested no conversation would be entered into.

At the police station, Craymer was left to ponder his fate in a cell while the duty solicitor was identified. He was out at lunch with a pretty, auburn-haired, blue-eyed trainee from the family law department who he considered the very embodiment of Celtic fire. So even when his office called him to say he was needed at the nick, where a man had been arrested on suspicion of conspiracy to murder, he decided lunch was the priority. And so it was that more than two hours passed before Ray was able to begin interviewing the man who had once been his prime suspect, who had seemingly been exonerated by a voice from the dead but remained 'a person of interest.'

After the formal introductions for the benefit of the whirring tape machine, Ray got straight down to it. 'Mr Craymer, I am investigating the kidnap, rape and subsequent murder of Kylie Morris, aged 12. You are here because I have reason to believe you may have information that is pertinent to that inquiry. Do you understand?'

'Yeah. But I know nowt.' The arrogance beginning to rise again.

'Your brother. Tell me about him. What's his name? Where does he live? What's his job? That kind of thing.'

'Brother? You're barking up the wrong tree mate.' Smugness now on top of the arrogance. 'I haven't got a brother.'

'What would be your reaction,' Ray began gently, 'if I was to tell you that I can prove you do have a brother? Only a half-brother, granted, but a brother nonetheless.'

Craymer stared blankly.

'You have different fathers but the same mother. Or are there more than two of you? Is that why you look puzzled? Mother put it about a bit did she?'

It was a question designed to trigger a response and it succeeded.

'You bastard. You leave my mother out of this. She was a decent woman. My Dad was killed when I was young and she got married again.'

Now it's working. Now he's starting to talk, thought Ray.

'OK, now that we've cleared that up. What about your brother? Like I said, I know you've got one. You just need to tell me about him. It's in your own interests.'

Craymer glanced sideways at the duty lawyer, who had half a mind on the trainee he had had to leave more hurriedly than he wanted. The lawyer nodded imperceptibly, indicating that Craymer should answer the officer's questions.

'Yeah, OK. I have got a brother. He's called Carl. Carl Higham. Higham was my step-dad's name see.'

'Yes, I understand how it works,' said Ray. 'But where can I find him.'

'He'll be at work.'

Ray couldn't decide whether Craymer was doing his best to be obstructive while appearing to be helpful or whether he was genuinely dumb, so he ventured: 'And where might that be?'

'All over the place,' replied Craymer.

'Alright. Let me put it another way,' said Ray, still controlling his patience. 'What does he do for a job?'

'He fixes old engineering machinery. Lathes and drilling machines. Stuff like that.'

At least the answer tied in with the forensic findings. He was on the right track.

'And where does he carry out that work?' asked Ray.

'I've already told you. All over the place.'

'But he must have a base that he operates from.'

Craymer let out an audible sigh. 'Yeah. Yeah, he does. But I don't know where it is.'

'Don't give me that,' said Ray, the first cracks in his patience beginning to appear. 'He's your brother. You must speak to him; tell each other what you're up to. You must know.'

'No. I don't,' insisted Craymer. 'At least, not proper.'

'What do you mean "not proper"?'

'I know he has a place where he keeps all his stuff. An old barn or shippon or something, I'm not sure. Out Bingley way.'

Ray had decided that his first instinct was correct. Craymer was being obstructive while pretending to co-operate but he also decided to continue on the same tack.

'And what might this little enterprise be called? What does he call his business?'

'It's not called 'owt. It's just him. He doesn't advertise or 'owt. He has his regulars and anything else comes in by word of mouth.'

'What's his phone number?'

'He doesn't have one.'

'Mobile?'

'He has one of them but I don't know the number.'

'So just how do you two communicate? I presume you do speak to each other?

'Yeah. He comes round to my place sometimes. Or I go to his.'

'So you do know where he lives then?' Ray moved his body forward across the desk and stared deeply into Craymer's eyes.

'I never said I didn't. You haven't asked me where he lives.'

Ray realised Craymer was right. He had been so focussed on finding out where Carl Higham might have imprisoned his victims that he had lost sight of the basics.

'Alright then Mr Craymer. What is your brother, Carl Higham's home address?'

Craymer sighed again and gave an address in the Little Horton area of Bradford.

'Thank you Mr Craymer. I think that will be all for now,' said Ray, with forced politeness.

'Does that mean I can go?' asked Craymer.

'Definitely not. You will be remanded in custody pending further inquiries.'

Five minutes later Ray was briefing his team, bringing all of them up to date on the developments and detailing Jan Holroyd, Mark Blake and Paul Prendergast to arrest Carl Higham and search his home.

'This needs to be done properly, so get a search warrant,' he told them. 'Take a couple of uniforms to help the search and keep nosy neighbours out of the way. You're looking for anything, I repeat anything, that can tie Higham to either of the murder victims and anything that might give us a lead to the location of this workshop his brother claims he has, somewhere in the Bingley area. But don't let the Bingley connection blind you to any other location. Craymer might be lying. It could be anywhere. Good luck. And keep me informed.'

The house in Little Horton had something of a familiar appearance to Mark Blake and Paul Prendergast. Like his brother's home, Carl Higham's house was, to say the least, neglected. The window frames that were visible at the front of the terraced property were rotten. The front door had not seen a paint brush for years and what had once been a glossed finish, possibly an attractive shade of blue, was now dull, flat and lifeless. A new, untreated piece of timber about six inches deep had been screwed across the bottom, probably, Blake thought, to keep the rotting timbers together. There was no knocker but, incongruously, the number 83 stood out in what appeared to be fairly new, black painted wrought iron.

Jan Holroyd wrinkled her nose in expectation of conditions on the other side as she banged hard on the door. After her second attempt went unanswered, she turned to the uniformed constable standing behind her. 'Open it,' she said.

The heavy Wam-Ram easily burst open the insubstantial lock but the timber was so badly decayed, the door jamb also splintered inwards under its weight. The three detectives, all wearing the regulation stab vests, charged in shouting 'Police' but managed only a few steps before Jan, who was in the lead, stopped dead.

'Christ. It smells like a fucking zoo,' she coughed, her hand to her mouth as she tried in vain not to inhale the unmistakable aroma of captive cats. With the front door now shattered and gaping, there was a veritable stampede of the creatures from every corner of the house. Blake would later claim he counted at least 10. In the kitchen a litter tray was overflowing, obviously unchanged for a considerable time, and piles of excrement and puddles of urine dotted the floor.

'This is fucking disgusting. What sort of arsehole lives like this,' Jan wondered out loud to no one in particular.

Dirty dishes were piled in the sink, awash in a grey, greasy scum that might once have been hot water. On the small, plastic-topped table, a slice of bread had turned green and an open jar of jam had developed a culture, instantly reminding Prendergast of a favourite joke about the difference between Australia and a pot of yoghurt.

'OK. I know it's going to be a shit job — literally — but let's get on with it,' said Jan. 'You two start down here and I'll have a look upstairs.' Pulling on a pair of blue Latex gloves from her pocket, she turned to the two uniformed officers and said: 'You make sure no one comes in and you, come with me.'

She was no more than four or five steps from the bottom when she found her way barred by a giant cat which had silently and ominously appeared at the top of the staircase. Its grubby, matted, shaggy brown coat served only to increase its bulk and its fearsome aspect as it fixed the two strangers through piercing, electric blue eyes. For several seconds the police officers and the monster were perfectly still, each eyeing the other until suddenly the cat rocked back on its haunches and began swiping the air with fearsome looking claws, hissing and spitting as it did so.

Jan was transfixed, uncertain what to do, when the young constable withdrew his baton, extended it to its full length and hurled it up the stairs. It bounced off the wall immediately behind the cat's head and rattled down the stairs with such a noise the terrified animal let out an ear-splitting screech and made a bee-line for the front door.

'Thanks. I hope we don't see that bastard again,' she said, relieved at not having had to do anything that might have brought her into contact with the beast, which she reckoned was bigger than some terriers she'd had known.

'Anytime sarge,' said the PC. 'I don't like bloody cats at the best of times.'

At the top of the staircase, the main bedroom opened directly off to the left. To the right, a short landing led to a smaller bedroom and a bathroom. In the ceiling, a small trapdoor looked like it gave access to the roof space.

In the main bedroom, Jan was amazed to find an antique brass bedstead which, like the rest of the house, was badly in need of care and attention. But whatever attraction it might have held was quickly dispelled by the musty aroma of unwashed bedding and human sweat that arose from it. She tried to open the window but the sash would not move and obviously had not been opened for some considerable time.

She carefully peeled back the bedclothes to reveal nothing except that Higham — she assumed this was his bed — preferred to sleep on the right hand side. Alongside the bed was a cheap cabinet on which were an old-fashioned clockwork alarm and a small bottle of proprietary indigestion tablets. Inside it was a collection of well-thumbed pornographic magazines, graphically depicting all manner of sexual behaviour but none of it indicating a predilection for young girls. A similarly cheap chest of drawers contained male underwear and socks, the majority of which Jan recognised as being a supermarket brand, and some tee-shirts.

In the wardrobe there were three or four shirts, a threadbare dark suit and an imitation tweed sports jacket. Under a dry-cleaner's plastic covering and in stark contrast to the other clothes in the room, was an immaculate, dark blue, traditional Crombie woollen overcoat with its trademark velvet collar. On the wardrobe floor were a pair of black shoes and a pair of brown ones.

Jan was just about to start a more minute examination of the room when the young constable called to her from the smaller bedroom he had been searching. 'Sarge, you need to see this.'

She entered the room to find him standing holding a drawer he had pulled from a small chest of four that was positioned against the wall, opposite a single bed.

Taped to the back of the drawer with duct tape were two small plastic bags. And in each bag was a lock of hair. One was dark, so dark it could have been black. But the other was a vivid, fiery red. The colour of red that was once Kylie Morris's crowning glory.

CHAPTER 19

Jan stared, horror stricken, at the two pathetic parcels. She had seen worse things in her career, far worse, but it was the knowledge that these were bundles of children's hair and that he had taken the time to cut them and save them and hide them away like precious jewels that turned her stomach. She felt the bile rising in her throat and fought the urge to vomit. It was several seconds before she was able to speak, but when she did she remained, outwardly at least, calm and in control.

'OK. I think that's all the proof we need,' she said to the constable. 'Put it back where you found it and we'll get the crime scene investigators in. In the meantime I think we've done up here. Let's see what's happening downstairs.'

In the front room, they found Blake and Prendergast crouched in a corner, examining a random pile of papers. 'It looks like our Mr Higham is a very methodical man,' said Blake looking up. 'His method is to chuck everything on this pile, no matter what it is. There's all sorts here. Takeaway menus, bills, bank statements, letters, you name it, it's here. Some of the stuff's been opened, some of it's not. What we're looking for may well be here, but if it is, it's buried.'

'Alright then. Bag the lot of it and let's take it back to the office,' said Jan. 'We're getting the crime scene bods in because we've just found two plastic bags with blonde hair in them taped to the back of a drawer. We'll let them finish wading through this shit and we'll go through all these papers at the nick.'

The DCI's office door stood wide open, so Detective Constable Peter Barnes gave it no more than a cursory tap and didn't even stop walking as he entered. 'Boss, we've just got an e-mail from GMP, that I think might interest you,' he said.

'Oh, and what makes you think that Barnsey?' asked Ray, his Fenland accent distinct.

'It's related to that little girl that's missing in Salford,' Barnes replied. 'It's a couple of ANPR pictures from Birch services, where they found her school uniform. They show a white van being driven by a man. There's no sign of anybody else but the thing is, the registration number matches a double-decker bus. In Leeds.'

'And you think this could be our man, do you? Ray asked.

'Well, it's possible. The first picture shows the van driving onto the eastbound service area. The second one shows him leaving four minutes later. Thing is, he's leaving by the back exit. He could be doubling back.'

'Interesting. He was there long enough to dump a kid's school uniform,' said Ray. 'Are there any more images from Birch that might give us a clue which way he went?'

'Unfortunately not,' he told his boss. 'I've spoken to the site manager and she says they only have CCTV in retail trading areas like the forecourt. There's no CCTV on the car parks on either side of the motorway.'

'What about images from the traffic cameras on the motorway?'

Barnes felt the flush of embarrassment creeping over his cheeks. It hadn't occurred to him to ask.

On another day and in a different mood, Ray could have exploded and delivered a lecture to the under-performing detective about initiative and standards and being thorough. But today he let the error slip by, recognising the young man's discomfort and in the knowledge that it was not a mistake he was ever likely to make again.

'Get onto to it straight away,' he said. 'See how far we can track this van. It might give us a lead as to where he was heading.'

Just as Barnes got back to his desk, secretly counting his lucky stars, Jan Holroyd, Blake and Prendergast returned, each carrying a large plastic bag stuffed with papers. Without a word of explanation, Jan tipped the contents of her sack onto her desk, sat down with a sigh and began the trawl through the detritus of one man's life. Behind her, Blake and Prendergast did the same.

'What's going on? Have we opened a recycling plant?' Ray asked, his curiosity aroused by the three piles of paper.

Jan explained the task and described the discovery of the hidden locks of hair. 'I've asked the crime scene investigators to fast track the forensics on the hair samples we found and on the cat hair. There was tons of it so hopefully we should get a match,' she explained.

Before Ray could say anything, his mobile began to vibrate in his pocket. 'Mr Wilson, it's Norman Marr at GMP,' the voice said. 'I thought you might like to know we've found her. We found Samantha Lowe. She's safe and well and unharmed, apart from being very cold. She's being checked over at hospital as we speak. Her parents are with her.'

Relief flooded through Ray, a feeling, almost, as if it was his own child that had been found. He was pleased Samantha had been found, but he was even more pleased that Kate's ordeal had ended. He didn't give a thought to Peter.

'That's great news Mr Marr,' he said. 'Where did you find her?'

'A couple of Community Support Officers found her early this morning,' he replied. 'She was asleep under a bench in a little park at the bottom of St John Street in the centre of Manchester. As yet, we've no idea what she was doing there but she told the CSOs she'd walked from Stockport. Quite a feat for such a young girl.'

'I think I know why she have been in that area,' said Ray, the street name instantly bringing back memories of Dr Miriam Tabor and the Sky-Scraper Woman. 'She underwent a course of therapy with a psychologist who practises in that street, a woman by the name of Tabor. Samantha seemed to trust her. Perhaps she was trying to see her.'

'That's a good thought. I'll get A Division to speak to the good doctor.'

'Best of luck with that,' said Ray, remembering her apparent intransigence.

That night, for the first time in weeks, Karen visited him again. Aided by a couple of very large glasses of his favourite single malt, Ray had fallen asleep in front of the television trying to watch the latest episode of an American spy thriller. In his dreams he saw her as she was when they first met: prim, efficient, reserved almost, but always in control. Then he saw her as he had come to know her: still efficient and in control but also loving, caring, funny. And then he saw her as she was the last time he had seen her: laid out on a mortuary slab, her beautiful face pulverised, her beautiful body shattered and broken, the way it had been left by a tearaway in a stolen car.

In his subconscious mind, he cried out to her; cried out in his grief. He woke with a start, staring around the room in the hope of finding something, some sign that he knew was not there and realised he had been dreaming. She will always be there, he thought. No matter where I go or what I do, she will always be with me.

Ray switched out the lights, went upstairs and had a hot shower. He climbed into bed and opened the book he was reading at the marked page. He read the same long paragraph three times before the book tumbled from his grasp and sleep came to him again. Karen did not.

Next morning, an air of expectation hung over the Major Incident Team office. They had a suspect. They knew his name. They knew where he lived. They just couldn't find him. But each and every member of the team also knew that the moment was at hand; that the breakthrough they so desperately needed was close. But still the morning dragged by, the unusual silence punctuated by the constant rustle of paper as six detectives shared the task of reading every single piece of paper recovered from Carl Higham's home. The occasional oath or frustrated sigh were the only other sounds. Even the telephone had stopped ringing.

The clock was ticking towards 1pm and thoughts were beginning to wander towards lunch. The days when it would have been spent in the local pub were long gone. Today the choice was between grabbing a quick bite in the canteen or a plastic-wrapped sandwich and a chocolate biscuit at the desk. Most of the squad were leaning towards the latter. And then it all happened at once.

The forensic lab phoned through their preliminary report and even as Ray was listening carefully to the information being given to him, there was a cry of 'Gotcha!' from the back of the squad room. Hanging up, Ray decided to impart his news first.

'Well ladies and gentlemen,' he began, mockingly formal. 'According to the forensic lab, the locks of hair found in bags at Carl Higham's home are a DNA match with Kylie Morris and Zoe Clayton. However, none of the extensive number of cat hairs recovered from the house match those found on the victims, which to my mind indicates only that he didn't take either of the girls there. We still need to find him urgently. Now Barnsey, what are you shouting about?'

'This Guv,' replied the young detective, waving a crumpled piece of paper in the air. 'It's an invoice from the water company for the installation of a water meter in a barn at a farm in Micklethwaite.'

A broad smile split Ray's face. 'Good work Barnsey,' he said. 'Now people, let's find out what this barn has to offer us. We need a search warrant and back up. We'd better have a dog handler as well. Jan, Blake, Prendergast and Barnes, you'll be with me. Two unmarked cars. And I want all vehicles to make a silent approach. I don't want him scared off before we get there.'

Frank Fisher still described himself as a farmer to anyone who cared to ask, but it had been a long, long time since he last had cattle to care for and even longer since he last tried to grow anything — and that was only potatoes. These days, it was the farm buildings that earned his income. He had converted the old shippon into livery stables for horses, which, at £75 a week each, brought in much more money than farming ever did. His biggest barn had been turned into six small units, each of which was rented out to a variety of self-employed people. One of them was occupied by a sculptor. God knew how he managed to make money but he always paid his rent on time. Another was used by a bloke who called himself a 'rustic carpenter.' He made stuff like garden benches and trellis and used the off-cuts to make nesting boxes for birds, selling the left-overs as kindling to people who owned log-burning stoves. He wasn't quite sure what went on in the other units and, if he was honest, he didn't ask too many questions, as long as the rent was paid on time. Yes, farming had been a good life for Frank Fisher. But being a landlord was a better one.

It was only when he turned into his farmyard off the narrow country lane that he realised it was full of police vehicles. There were two big vans with metal grills that could be pulled down over the windscreen, a smaller van that said 'Dog Unit' on the side and two unmarked cars. He saw about a dozen burly officers, dressed in black from head to toe, wearing what looked like flak jackets and military-style helmets. The occupant of the back of the dog unit was making his presence heard.

'What the fuck's going on?' he asked everyone and no one as he climbed out of his Land Rover.

At the sound of the question, a well-built man, who looked like he could be in charge, turned and walked towards him.

'And you are?' asked Ray.

'This is my farm. What the fuck's going on?'

'I am Detective Chief Inspector Raymond Wilson and we have a warrant to search these premises in connection with a murder enquiry Mr ...?'

'Fisher. Frank Fisher,' the farmer replied. 'I don't know anything about any murder.'

'In particular we are looking for a man by the name of Carl Higham, who we believe may use this property in connection with his business,' explained Ray, ignoring Fisher's protestation of innocence. 'He repairs and renovates engineering equipment. Lathes, that kind of thing.'

For a few seconds, Fisher's brow furrowed in puzzlement. 'Ah, him,' he finally said, as if a light had suddenly been switched on in a dark corner of his memory. 'He used to have one of the units in the barn but he left about a year ago. Found himself somewhere new.'

Ray tried to disguise his disappointment. 'Do you know where he went?' he asked.

'Not really. He just said he'd found a place closer to home that was more suited to his needs.'

'And you didn't ask him for a forwarding address?'

'No,' answered Fisher. 'To be honest, I was never keen on the bloke. There was always something about him. I couldn't put my finger on it but I just knew I didn't like him. I was glad to see the back of him, between you and me.'

'Do you mind if we have a look round the place he used to have?' Ray was now desperate for clues; anything that might give him a lead to where Higham was right now.

'Be my guest,' said Fisher. 'There's a new bloke in there now. Something to do with paint. But there's nothing left from when Higham had it. He took everything. Except his fucking cat.'

'Cat? He left a cat?'

Fisher had no idea why this copper, who said he was investigating a murder, should be so interested in a bloody moggy.

'Yeah. Fucking great big thing. And wild; wild as they come,' he said.

'Is it still here?' asked Ray.

'Nah. It's well dead,' Fisher said. 'It attacked my young grandson one day. Gave him a right good clawing, so I shot the bastard.'

After such a promising start, Ray's day was turning increasingly bad. 'I don't suppose you buried it here did you?' he asked, more in hope than expectation.

'There wasn't a right lot left to bury after I gave it both barrels of a 12-bore. I chucked the bits on a rubbish fire we had. Why?'

'It doesn't matter,' sighed Ray. 'Which unit did Higham have?'

'Number five. The one in the far corner.'

'Thank you for your co-operation Mr Fisher. We'll just take a quick look if you don't mind and then we'll leave you in peace.'

As he turned away towards his team, he saw from the looks on their faces that they had heard every word of his conversation.

'Looks like this is a dead end but we'll search Higham's old unit anyway,' he told them. 'Blake, Prendergast, use one of the support teams and see if you can find anything that might just be remotely interesting in there. We'll see you back at the ranch. Jan, Barnes, you come back with me.'

Just before he closed the driver's door, Ray heard mutterings of 'This is a waste of bloody time,' from among the uniforms. He pretended not to hear.

At the same time the police were raking through his old unit, Carl Higham was trying to work out what was the matter with him. Today should have been the day; the day when he began his fun again. But for some reason he had lost the urge. He didn't know why but he didn't want to do anything to the terrified little girl he had well and truly secreted away. He didn't want to hear her cry from sheer fear; he didn't want to hear her beg to go home; he didn't want to hear her plead for her mummy and he didn't want to hurt her. That didn't mean he was going to let her go. He would have to kill her sometime because, apart from anything else, she had seen his face: it just wouldn't be today. He would go home and spend the day drinking cider and vodka while he watched his collection of sexually violent DVDs. That should restore his appetite. His young victim could die another day.

What he would do, though, was make sure she was alright, by which he meant he would check she was still securely bound. He'd feed her some tomato soup, even take her to the toilet. And then he would lock her away again until he was ready.

Ray was at his desk reading through the forensic reports for the umpteenth time, trying to build a mental picture of the man he hunted, the man he now believed was Carl Higham, when Jan and the rest of the team arrived back from Frank Fisher's farm. He looked up as Jan knocked on his open door. 'Well?' was all he said.

'Like we suspected guv, absolutely nothing that linked to Carl Higham,' she replied. 'We did have a bit of a result though. One of the uniform lads opened a can of paint, probably because the guy who's in there now was being a bit of a prat, and guess what? It was full of cannabis. So we opened some more and found even more cannabis and some cocaine.'

'Good work,' said Ray. 'Where's the guy now?'

'Downstairs in a cell, waiting for the Drug Squad. They're very keen to talk to him about the penalties for being convicted of possession with intent to supply and no doubt ask him some questions about his supplier.'

'At least something's come of our little visit,' said Ray. 'If only we could find where Higham has gone.'

Jan saw the stare of a distant horizon cross his face as he turned to gaze out across the city. 'He can't be far away, I know it,' a thought almost involuntarily murmured. 'We just need a break.'

Just then a uniformed police woman, who Jan recognised as Carol Braun, an ambitious young officer who desperately wanted to join the Major Incident Team, knocked on the door.

' 'Scuse me sir,' she began, 'I've been looking through this traffic camera stuff that Barnsey ordered and I think you might be interested in some of the bits I've found.'

Ray turned back, the faraway look gone. 'OK. Show me what you've got,' he said, turning his laptop towards her. He noticed that enthusiasm was written all over her face.

'Well sir, the pictures from the ANPR camera at Birch services show him leaving the eastbound site through the back entrance that's supposed to be for permit holders only,' said Braun. 'Then the ANPR camera at the back entrance to the westbound site shows him entering a couple of minutes later. He's obviously driven back over the motorway.'

Ray and Jan watched as two grainy still images showed a small white van carrying the registration number they now knew Higham was using, flickered across the screen. Each was stamped with the camera's location and the time and date the image was captured. The date matched Anne-Marie Doherty's disappearance.

Braun continued. 'The next time we see him is a few minutes later, heading back towards Manchester before he turns off onto the M60 but then he turns off the motorway at the first junction.' More images, this time of moving traffic, tracked the van's progress.

'We then lose him completely until he's picked up by a camera on Scammonden Dam. He must have worked his way back across country and rejoined the motorway. Anyway, there are a couple more shots of him before he leaves the M62 and joins the M606 towards Bradford. At the end of the M606, he turns right onto the ring road and then we see him next at the Dudley Hill roundabout, where he could have turned left towards the city centre but he doesn't.'

The pictures on screen showed the white van approach the huge roundabout in the nearside lane, apparently about to make a left turn, but at the last minute the driver accelerated across the path of a motorcyclist coming from his right and went around the roundabout.

'He takes the next turn and carries on along the ring road,' explained Braun, 'but it's the next bit of film that's interesting.'

She said nothing more but allowed Ray and Jan to see for themselves as the film showed the white van in a line of traffic pulling away from a set of traffic lights. Just as the vehicle reached the top of the screen, Braun said, 'Now, just watch this.' It took a keen eye to spot that the driver had put on the van's right indicator. And it took an even keener eye to see that the fraction of vehicle remaining on screen was turning right into a side street.

'Excellent Braun, bloody excellent,' said Ray. 'How long did it take to piece that together?'

'Only about eight hours sir. There were four of us.'

'Well, give them all my congratulations,' he said, mentally calculating that it had taken 32 man-hours of eye-aching scrutiny of grainy, fast-moving images to reach this point. 'Now, do we know exactly where he turned off?'

Braun replied: 'Yes sir. It's a residential street. The problem is that we lose him again after that. There's just no trace of him.'

Jan added: 'It's the opposite side of the city to where he lives so I'd bet it's where he's got his new place.'

'Is there any industrial property in that area?' Ray asked Braun.

'Not in that immediate locality but there's a warren of streets that lead all over the place, if you know where you're going,' she answered.

Even though it was still fairly nebulous, it was the best lead they had had since Higham was identified and Ray could not afford any mistakes. He ordered every police officer in the city be issued with the van's false registration number and told to report any sightings but not to approach the occupant. He also asked for increased patrols in the area to the east of the ring road in the area in which Higham's van had vanished.

He glanced at his watch and realised that it was a few minutes after six-thirty. He also realised that his squad room was still full, his team heads down, still working through every little detail. Again.

Tugging on his jacket, he called to the room, 'Right people. Enough for today. Beers are on me, come on.' And then, almost as an afterthought he added, 'And Jan, ask Constable Braun if she'd like to join us.'

There was a time, many years before Ray arrived in the city, that Bradford's skyline was dominated by mill chimneys, some of them plain, functional things, others more elaborate, conspicuous displays of the fortunes the textile barons were making from the fine worsted wool that thousands of citizens bent their backs daily to produce. Most of the mills worked around the clock — the lights blazing from their myriad of windows giving the impression of a vast armada of ships at sea — as raw wool was scoured, carded, spun and woven into the fabric that was the best in the world and graced the backs of kings and commoners, albeit wealthy ones, alike.

But today only a handful of mills remain, all converted into apartments, offices or cavernous showrooms. The vast majority were long since demolished and the sites developed as housing estates, shopping centres or industrial parks. A few survived virtually untouched but semi-derelict: broken windows unreplaced, paintwork faded and peeling, weeds growing from blocked gutters, the handful of out-buildings rented out to small businesses, many of them one-man-bands, but with a general air of neglect hanging over them, sad reminders of what once had been.

As darkness began to fall over the city, it was to just such a place that Ted McGarvie and his dog Buddy were headed. Ted had spent a lifetime patrolling the city's streets as a police dog handler. Never ambitious, he had neither sought nor won promotion, content to spend his career at the bottom of the police ladder dealing with — as he described them — 'proper people with proper problems.' He had been on the beat when the notorious multiple murderers The Black Panther and The Yorkshire Ripper, both of whom lived in Bradford, focussed the international spotlight on the city he loved.

But when retirement called, Ted soon discovered that his pension never quite stretched far enough to allow him to live in the manner he wished, so he took a part-time job as a security guard. His police training stood him in good stead and it wasn't long before he was teamed up with Buddy and the pair now spent four nights a week keeping a close eye on other people's property. The new owners of the former mill he was approaching were concerned at the amount of lead, copper wiring, stone and other instantly saleable material that was regularly going missing, so had brought in a security company. It was Ted's job to visit the place twice a night to check that the doors were still locked, no more windows had been broken and that the place remained as secure as it could be.

A full moon, flitting in and out of scudding cloud, cast occasional shadows across the old mill yard as Ted parked the van and let Buddy out of the back, giving the Alsatian a couple of minutes to go off and relieve himself before calling him to heel and clipping on his tracker lead.

He began his patrol at what used to be the mill's main entrance. Satisfied that the door was secure and the lock still in place and working, he moved on. A complete circuit of the five storey building brought him back to the yard with its small collection of out-buildings, one of which, he knew, used to be a small car workshop. He knew that because he used to get his car serviced there by a pot-bellied Welshman he knew only as Brynn. Then, one day, Brynn wasn't there and Ted had to look elsewhere.

I wonder whatever happened to Brynn, he thought as he crossed the yard, Buddy walking faithfully to heel, the lead slack in his hand. He always did a good job and never charged the earth. Not like some of those buggers out there today.

He was still several feet from the door as he shone his torch to check the lock. As he grasped it, he felt Buddy tense up. He put down a reassuring hand and realised the dog's hackles had risen. 'What is it boy? What's disturbing you?' he asked in the manner that even otherwise sensible people adopt when talking to their dogs.

He rattled the lock to satisfy himself that the double doors — which he knew from experience were the only way in and out — really were secured and that there was no one inside. Buddy began to bark but suddenly fell silent, sat down and cocked his head to one side. He's heard something, Ted thought, bending his ear close to the door himself. At first he heard nothing. Then there was a rustling that could easily have been a rat, at which Buddy began to whimper softly. There's something in there that's disturbing him, Ted said to himself and then out loud authoritatively, 'OK. Security. I know you're in there. Come out now.'

There was no response, no sound except for Buddy's continued whimpering.

Putting his ear to the door a second time, Ted thought he heard a sound; a distant, muffled sound; a sound that could have been crying. Without moving he called out, 'Hello.' This time he heard it for sure. It was unmistakably a voice. A little girl's voice.

And it was sobbing, 'Help me.'

CHAPTER 20

Usually on the Ordsall estate, a midnight visit from the police meant only one thing — trouble — but tonight was different. The two young police officers were delivering good news, although the neighbours who watched from behind gaps in the curtains, acutely aware that Anne-Marie was missing, had no way of knowing that.

Despite the hour, all the lights were blazing in the Docherty's house as the adults inside tried to console one another; to tell each other everything would be alright; that Anne-Marie had probably only got lost. An overflowing ashtray, empty lager cans and an almost-empty bottle of cheap vodka were silent witnesses to the family's anguish.

And then Billy Frayn, Anne-Marie's grandfather, saw the patrol car glide to a halt, its presence triggering only grief and despair, a sure signal to those who loved the little girl the most that the unthinkable was about to manifest itself.

Bernard Docherty simply held open the front door while the two policemen entered. Christine Docherty sat on the sofa, wringing a once-white handkerchief between trembling hands, her eyes rimmed red by tears, wretchedness etched into her face.

'Have you found her?' she begged before either officer had the chance to speak.

'Yes. And...' began the older of the two.

'Oh my God.' The wail launched from deep inside. 'She's dead isn't she? I know it. She's dead.' The last words spoken so quickly they merged into one unbroken syllable, recognisable only by those trained to deal with grief.

'No Mrs Docherty, she's not,' the policeman said quickly. 'That's what we're here to tell you. Anne-Marie is alive and unhurt.'

More tears welled in the eyes of the three adults and the two men moved, almost protectively, to Christine's side. Within seconds all three were hugging each other, grinning widely and jumping with joy.

The officer murmured to his younger companion, 'Go and see if you can put a brew on Duane. I think they need it.'

'Right then,' he said. 'I'm PC Ben Moores and my colleague in there is PC Duane Morgan. We don't have a lot of detail but I can tell you Anne-Marie was found earlier this evening in an old mill in Bradford.'

'What? Bradford in east Manchester?' interjected Billy Frayn.

'No sir. Bradford in West Yorkshire,' replied PC Moores patiently.

'But how did she get there?' asked Christine.

'Like I said, we don't have too many details. All I know is that right now Anne-Marie is in hospital having a check-up to make sure she's OK.'

'But Bradford,' said Christine, struggling to comprehend how her 10 year-old came to be on the other side of the Pennines. 'How are we going to get to Bradford? We haven't got a car or anything.'

'Mrs Docherty. Don't worry,' said Moores. 'We have and we'll take you.'

By the time Ray reached the old mill, Anne-Marie was in hospital, the building that had been her prison was sealed off and what seemed like an army of people in protective suits, face masks and over-shoes were swarming all over it. He had been alerted to Ted McGarvie's discovery by the duty inspector in the control room who, aware of the request that every officer on the street be given the registration number of a vehicle that was wanted in connection with a missing 10 year-old girl, thought it politic to call.

The first person he saw when he stepped from the patrol car that had been sent to collect him was Jan Holroyd and, to his surprise, standing by her side was Barnsey. Ray decided not to comment and simply asked, 'OK. What have we got?'

'It's that little girl that was reported missing from Salford,' replied Jan. 'Security guard found her. Actually, he heard her crying. But he's ex-job and had the sense not go inside. He put in a three nines call and two of our guys went in and brought her out.'

'She's alright?' asked Ray, somehow managing to make the question sound more like a statement.

Jan said, 'The lads said she had a few grazes and bruises from where she'd been tied up but apart from that she appeared unhurt. She's in hospital now being given a full check-up and the doctors have been alerted to the possibility she could have been sexually assaulted. So far, we've heard nothing back.'

Ray thought for a moment. 'Right Barnsey. First off, thanks for turning out tonight. I appreciate it. Now, I want you to go to the hospital, make sure the doctors doing the examinations know you're there and ring me the second there's any news.'

'Right boss,' was all he said, but as he walked away, it occurred to Jan that he stood a little bit taller.

The next question was aimed at Jan, 'Who's in charge of scene investigations?'

'Barbara Myerscough, I believe,' Jan replied. 'That's her over there.'

The all-enveloping protective suits and face masks completely disguised any gender specifics, making the team of investigators indistinguishable one from another. It was only when Ray got close to the person Jan had indicated that he saw big, soft green eyes with just a hint of make-up behind her clear protective glasses.

By way of introduction he said, 'Hi, I'm Detective Chief Inspector Ray Wilson, MIT, and I believe you already know Detective Sergeant Jan Holroyd. Can we have a look inside?' As ice-breakers go, it was probably a bit brusque but both Ray and the scientist recognised that this was not the time for niceties and pleasantries.

'You can,' she answered. 'But you need to get suited up and don't walk off the steps. And for God's sake don't touch anything. There's still a lot of work to do in there.'

'You are aware that this is potentially also the scene of at least one very violent assault that led to the death of a young girl and possibly the murder of another?' ventured Ray.

'Yes I am,' Barbara Myerscough responded. 'That's why I don't want your bloody big size tens trampling all over the place. You can have a quick look and then we need to get on with our job, if you don't mind Chief Inspector.'

Dressed in their protective suits and masks, Ray and Jan became just two more unidentifiable people. Inside the workshop, large plastic steps had been placed on the floor to prevent contamination being walked in, even though everybody within was wearing plastic overshoes. Powerful arc lights lit the interior, revealing a long bench, to which were bolted two differently sized vices, and a well organised wall of tools with each tool clipped perfectly in its place. On the bench were parts of a machine, which neither police officer could recognise and off to one side stood a partly assembled lathe. The air was heavy with the smell of oil.

But it was the workshop floor that drew Ray and Jan's horrified attention.

Dug into the centre of the room was a pit, somewhere between five and six feet deep, with a set of steps leading down into it from one end. Over the pit hung a powerful chain operated block-and-tackle hoist, at the end of which was a large steel hook. Tied to the hook was a length of rope, with its ends fashioned into loops, just large enough to hold a small wrist.

'The sick fuck,' said Jan, giving voice to the thoughts of everybody in the place.

Carl Higham was in a good mood. A few cans of strong cider, a couple of sexually violent DVDs followed by a sound night's sleep had set him up just right. Today was going to be the day. And he was going to enjoy it.

The fact that his intended young victim was, at that moment, sitting up in a hospital bed being fussed over by her ecstatic parents, was not yet public knowledge. The layout of the old mill where she had been held was such that the police activity was hidden from view and anyway there were virtually no local residents left to call the local radio station to report 'something going on' — the very qualities that had attracted Higham to the location in the first place. Even if by some freak chance, news had leaked out, it was unlikely Higham would have heard it. His van radio was tuned to the kind of station where news runs a poor third to wall-to-wall music and the banal blabberings of its presenters.

He was singing along to a classic rock tune from his youth, beating out the rhythm on the steering wheel, as he made his approach to the mill. But as he turned into the yard his whole world turned to black as he found himself confronted by a host of vehicles — marked and unmarked police cars, crime scene vans and even an ambulance — and all the people they had brought. He braked to a halt, his mind racing. The entrance road he was on was too narrow to allow a rapid three-point turn.

He couldn't risk driving into the yard. His only option was to reverse, quietly and unseen.

But in his rush to escape, he crunched the gear selection with a metallic grinding sound that made him wince.

Fifty yards away, Jan Holroyd appeared to be the only person who had heard the noise. She glanced in his direction and immediately recognised the registration plate that actually belonged to a Leeds bus and which Higham had not thought to change.

'Boss, it's him,' she yelled, pointing at the retreating vehicle. 'It's Higham.'

Ray turned just in time to catch a glimpse of a headlight disappearing from view.

'Are you sure?' he said, excitement rising in his chest.

'Course I'm sure,' she shouted back and then added, 'Sorry boss.'

'Right, let's get after him. Come on.'

The pair jumped into the back of the patrol car that had brought Ray to the scene because he believed his very large sundowner scotch would have affected his ability behind the wheel. 'That's our man,' he barked at the driver. 'Get after him. And I want back-up. Get the helicopter up. And don't lose him.'

The officer in the passenger seat hit the electronic keypad that activated the car's blue lights and wailing siren. Then he picked up the radio microphone, called in to the force control room and calmly gave the car's location and the fact that they were in pursuit of a white van and repeated its registration number twice. He asked for back up from any available vehicles and requested that X-Ray Niner Niner — the helicopter's call sign — be scrambled.

Higham was in a blind panic, driving erratically, turning left and right with no real plan of where he was heading. He just wanted to escape. Suddenly he found himself at a junction and realised he was on the ring road that skirted around the city. For no other reason than it was the easiest option, he turned left and accelerated hard. A few minutes later he recognised the massive Dudley Hill roundabout and knew instantly that the motorway was within easy reach. He shot down the dual-carriageway and sliced across a line of slower moving traffic in the inside lane to reach the M606, which led to the M62 trans-Pennine motorway that linked the west coast of England to the east coast and which, he believed, offered him his best chance of freedom.

He hadn't counted on the all-seeing eye that was X-Ray Niner Niner which, even as he pelted along the M606, was 2,000 feet above him relaying his position to force control and all the vehicles that had joined the chase. He joined the M62 heading east, weaving in and out of the lines of traffic, causing anger and consternation in equal measure, but still carefully watched from above.

By now another marked patrol car and two unmarked cars were in pursuit, blue lights flashing, sirens blaring, scything their way through the traffic to catch up with Ray who, according to the helicopter's observer, was now only a couple of miles behind the fleeing Higham. As the intersections with the A1 link road and the M1 motorway passed by Ray instructed the car's crew, 'Right, let's start slowing them down. Get the control room to reduce the speed.'

A few seconds later, the matrix signs on gantries above the carriageway began to light up. 'Queue ahead. Slow Down 50mph' the first ones said. Subsequent signs reduced the speed limit to 40mph and then 30mph.

Very few of the hundreds of vehicles hurtling eastwards actually obeyed the instruction, but enough of them reduced their speed to the point where traffic began to bunch up, which had the overall effect of slowing progress for everybody. It also allowed the other three police cars to catch up.

'Now all we have to do is find him,' said Ray. 'And when we do, I think we're going to have to use a hard stop.'

'A hard stop? Are you sure sir?' asked Jan.

'Well, he might stop if we asked him nicely,' replied Ray. 'But if I was him I'd take every chance I could to get away so I don't really think we have an alternative, do you?'

He read her silence as agreement and said to the car's observer, 'Tell the others what the plan is and when we catch up with him, you call the shots.'

It was two, maybe three miles further on that the observer suddenly called out, 'There he is,' and pointed at a white van in the nearside lane, sandwiched between two articulated lorries in a line of traffic that was moving along at more than 50mph, despite the matrix signs ordering 30mph.

'Target vehicle is a white Nissan van, registration number Yankee Alpha Zero Five Mike Bravo Golf,' the observer was saying into his radio. 'All acknowledge visual identification.' One by one the three pursuing cars gave acknowledgement.

'Romeo Papa Two Seven, you are lead vehicle,' was the next instruction. 'X-Ray One Zero, you take the offside. X-Ray Seven Six you take the nearside and we'll take the rear. Acknowledge.' Once again, the three cars radioed their understanding.

'Execute hard stop. Go.'

In a perfect world, the four cars would have surrounded the van, leaving the driver nowhere to go, and gradually brought him to a halt.

But the escaping van was so close to the lorry in front there was no room for Romeo Papa Two Seven to get in between them. Then, the flashing blue lights and blaring horns did their trick. The lorry driver, realising what was happening, suddenly accelerated, creating just enough space for the police car to slot in behind him. Higham too, recognised what was happening. He'd seen hard stops on those police pursuit programmes on the television and sure enough, he now had a marked car behind him, one in front of him and an unmarked car on his right. There was only one place left to go.

He swung the wheel violently to the left in the vain hope of getting away on the hard shoulder. But he hadn't reckoned on the presence of X-Ray Seven Six, which was charging along the hard shoulder concealed from his view by the van's extensive blind spot. The first Higham knew of the police car was a terrifyingly loud bang from the rear near quarter as the impact lifted the left rear wheel clear off the ground. The van, now on three wheels, rocketed up the embankment, scrabbling for grip but failing to find it.

There was a screech of brakes and a smell of burning rubber as other vehicles on the motorway tried to avoid becoming part of the unfolding scene.

Higham had a view of grass and earth coming closer then receding, followed by a brief snatch of sky and something that could have been lorry wheels as his van rolled over on to its side before crashing on to its roof across the hard shoulder. Even though he was hanging dazed and upside down in his seatbelt, the desire for flight was still foremost in his mind. Unthinking, he unfastened the belt, dropped a few inches head first onto the roof and crawled to freedom through the broken window. But freedom was short lived. He found himself lying on his back staring up at a uniformed policeman who, from his lowly position, looked like the tallest man he'd ever seen.

Impassively, but with remarkable politeness, the officer enquired, 'Are you injured at all, sir?'

Jan Holroyd, who had appeared at the officer's side, was less formal, 'Right pal, you're fucking nicked.'

While Higham was being formally arrested and processed, Ray used the time to make the telephone calls he knew he had to make. The first was to his counterpart in North Yorkshire CID to tell him a man suspected of murdering Kylie Morris had been arrested and suggesting they might also like to interview him in connection with the murder of Zoe Clayton.

The next call was to the parents of Kylie Morris to tell them of the development before they saw it on television or heard it on the radio. Although he only told them the man had been arrested on suspicion of murdering their daughter, he left them in little doubt that this was the man responsible.

His third call was the most difficult. He rang Kate Lowe on her mobile at work. The relief in her voice almost reached out across the airwaves and stroked his face.

'So, if Stephen Parke and Richard Fairfax are right, Samantha's problems should come to end,' he ventured. 'And if they do I've no doubt Fairfax in particular will be shouting it from the rooftops. That's something you should be prepared for.'

'I hadn't thought of that,' Kate replied. 'But surely they couldn't do that without our permission.'

'If they don't reveal your identity, I'm not sure they need it,' he said. 'They can write a paper for one of the big medical journals explaining the problems of an unnamed little girl and how they were resolved. At least if they do it that way you shouldn't get pestered by the media.'

Kate said: 'Yeah, I suppose that's one good thing. By the way, we found out why Samantha ran off into Manchester. She was going to see that psychologist Miriam Tabor. Apparently she remembered some kind of pit that Kylie was in and thought she'd better tell the doctor.'

The statement impressed him. Always sceptical of the theory of cellular memory, he was becoming more and more convinced of its validity.

'I didn't realise she was still seeing her.'

'Yes, she's been a few times now,' answered Kate. 'And it seems to be doing her some good. She still has the nightmares but she seems to coping with them much better.'

'Well, with luck, all that will be over now.'

'Yes, hopefully. And Ray, I just want to say how grateful we are for your help and understanding. You're a very kind man. But I guess this is goodbye eh?'

Ray felt the hot prickle of tears fill his eyes. 'It doesn't have to be,' he whispered through the emotion.

'Yes it does and you know it as well as I do,' she said. 'I was very flattered by your attentions but it wasn't me you wanted was it? It was someone else. That's why you kept calling me Karen. Whoever she was she means more to you than I would ever have done. And anyway, I love Pete. We're good together. I could never leave him, especially after what we've been through. So Ray, this really is goodbye. Please don't call me again.'

He just managed to say: 'Goodbye...Kate' before the line went dead.

That night Samantha Lowe slept soundly and untroubled for the first time in almost a year. At breakfast the following morning, Kate simply asked: 'Did you have a good night's sleep sweetheart?'

The little girl replied: 'Yes I did. Kylie came again but it was alright this time. She came to say everything was ok now. She said she wouldn't trouble me again but that she'd always be with me because I've got her heart.'

Kate and Peter just stared at each other, speechless.

Richard Fairfax had his white crow.

And in Bradford, two dirty, matted and un-fed cats went in search of vermin around the old mill where, until yesterday, they had been the companions of a man who occasionally gave them something to eat and drink.

The forensic evidence gathered in Higham's workshop was conclusive. DNA samples obtained from the rope over the pit matched both Kylie and Zoe Clayton. The length of timber he used to batter both girls was found hidden under a pile of rags and surrendered not only DNA matches to the victims but also a single, crystal-clear fingerprint that matched Higham's right index finger. But as far as Jan Holroyd was concerned, the icing on the cake was that cat hair found in the workshop matched those found on both girls' bodies. Meowplex was a winner.

Higham confessed to both murders but put the blame on his stepbrother who, he said, convinced him to kidnap and hold Kylie in revenge for being dumped by her mother. He was only supposed to keep her a couple of days. But then things got out of hand...

Ray at last allowed his thoughts to stray back to the sea and sailing and to the Whitby Yacht Club, where he had unfinished business to attend to. And a lot of bridges to rebuild.

37187766R00097

Printed in Great Britain
by Amazon